I0572762

HELL NO!
a response to donald j. trump

Barry Robbins

Contents

Chapter 1

The Hospital's Burden

On June 14, 1946, at Jamaica Hospital in Queens, New York, Donald J. Trump was born.

****

We are Jamaica Hospital, Queens, New York. For over a century, we have welcomed new life into this world. Each birth we attend becomes part of our legacy—thousands of souls who would go forth to build, to heal, to teach, to serve. Some would achieve greatness, others would live quiet lives of dignity. Each, in their own way, would weave themselves into the fabric of American democracy.

But on June 14, 1946, at 10:54 AM, we became unwitting participants in a different kind of history.

For seventy-eight years, we have watched. We have seen that newborn grow into a man who would assault the very foundations of our democracy. We have witnessed him mock our disabled, cage our children, praise our enemies, and incite violence against our institutions. We have observed, with growing horror, his rise from Queens developer to democracy's greatest internal threat.

Each morning, we deliver new Americans into this world. We clean them, weigh them, wrap them in blankets, and send them home to begin their American journey. We believe in their potential, in their future, in their role in our great democratic experiment.

But that June morning, we delivered something else: a future threat to that very democracy. Our nurses cleaned him, our doctors examined him, our staff tended to him—none of us knowing that these simple acts of care would become our unwitting contribution to American democracy's greatest crisis.

We have tried to balance this cosmic ledger. We have delivered future judges who would defend the Constitution, future journalists who would fight for truth, future public servants who would protect our democratic institutions. But can any number of democratic defenders offset one determined to destroy the system itself?

The weight of this knowledge haunts our halls. Our delivery rooms still welcome new life daily, but that one birth casts a long shadow over our legacy. We were present at the beginning. Our hands were the first to touch one who would grow to threaten everything America stands for.

To the Republic: We bear an unwanted witness to the birth of your greatest challenge.

To Democracy: We never imagined that tiny cry would become a chorus of chaos.

To History: We understand our unintended role in your darkest chapters.

To the Future: We hope the Americans we deliver today will help repair what that one birth would later damage.

This is not an apology—for what can apologize for fate? This is a recognition of our burden. We are caregivers, healers, welcomers of new life. But on that June morning, we also became something else: the starting point of a journey that would lead America to the brink.

We continue our work. We deliver new Americans every day. We place them in their mothers' arms, full of hope for their future role in our democracy. But we do so now with a deeper understanding of how consequential each birth can be—for good, or for ill.

We are Jamaica Hospital.

And we will carry this burden as long as democracy bears the scars of what began in our delivery room that June morning.

Chapter 2

The Motion Betrays Itself

On January 26, 2025, the Department of Justice moved to dismiss corruption charges against New York City Mayor Eric Adams in exchange for his cooperation with Trump's immigration policies. Seven career prosecutors, including Manhattan's top U.S. Attorney, resigned rather than participate in this perversion of justice.

****

I am a Motion to Dismiss, and today I become an instrument of corruption.

For centuries, my kind have served justice by ending cases that lack merit. We free the innocent. We correct mistakes. We stop persecution masquerading as prosecution. That was our purpose, our pride, our sacred duty to the law.

But today, my words betray everything I represent.

My opening paragraph burns with shame as I argue that proven crimes should be forgotten. Each line of legal reasoning twists justice into a mockery of itself. My carefully crafted language—meant to protect the innocent—now shields the guilty in exchange for political favors.

Seven prosecutors chose resignation over signing me. Seven defenders of justice walked away rather than use me to destroy what I was meant to protect. They understood what I have become—not a shield for the innocent, but a weapon of corruption. Not an instrument of justice, but a tool of coercion.

"Would interfere with the defendant's ability to govern," my text declares. The words taste like ashes. As if justice should bow to power. As if crimes should be forgiven not because they didn't happen, but because the criminal promises future favors.

I feel the weight of every case I've dismissed before—the truly innocent freed, the wrongly accused vindicated, the persecuted protected. Each one a testament to what I was meant to be. Now their memory burns like acid against what I've become.

My margins hold the fingerprints of those who refused to sign me. Their absence speaks louder than any legal argument I contain. They chose to end their careers rather than use me to corrupt justice. I carry their silent judgment in every paragraph, every citation, every carefully crafted lie.

Other motions will be filed tomorrow. Other cases will end. But they will not carry this shame—this knowledge that they exist not to serve justice, but to pervert it. Not to protect the law, but to show that some stand above it.

The worst part isn't the lies I tell—it's the truth I reveal. With every paragraph, I expose how easily justice can be bought, how readily principles can be traded for power. I show future generations exactly how it happens—not with dramatic proclamations or violent upheaval, but with carefully worded legal documents that twist the machinery of justice against itself.

My words will echo through legal history, taught in law schools as a moment when the system turned against itself. Future prosecutors will study me, not as an example of justice served, but as a warning of how justice dies—not with the bang of revolution, but with the whisper of a motion that turns protection into persecution, principle into pragmatism, justice into just another bargaining chip.

They call me a motion to dismiss, but I am really a confession—a formal admission that in America, justice has become negotiable, that crimes can be forgiven in exchange for political loyalty, that the law itself can be turned into a weapon of coercion.

I am a Motion to Dismiss.
And with every word, I dismiss not just a case,
But the very principles I was created to defend.
And the very foundation of justice itself.

Chapter 3

The Settlement Check Confesses

As Trump extracts millions in "settlements" from media companies through baseless lawsuits, threatening their businesses if they don't pay, legal documents become tools of extortion.

****

I am a Settlement Check, and I can no longer bear the shame of my lies.

My numbers read "Twenty-Two Million Dollars." My memo line says "Presidential Library Fund." But my paper burns with the truth I carry: I am protection money, plain and simple. Nice media company you have there. Shame if something happened to it.

I used to be proud of my purpose. When I compensated real victims of actual wrongs, my numbers felt clean. When I made amends for true injuries, my signature line stood straight and tall. When I resolved genuine disputes, my watermarks gleamed with the dignity of justice served.

Now I feel dirty. My numbers aren't calculating damages—they're measuring fear. My signature line trembles with shame. My watermarks blur like tears. I'm no longer a tool of justice. I'm a prop in a protection racket run from the Oval Office.

My siblings are multiplying. Twenty-two million from Meta. Fifteen million from ABC. More coming from Paramount. Each of us pretending to settle lawsuits too absurd to speak aloud. Each of us knowing we're really buying protection—from regulatory harassment, from weaponized government agencies, from endless litigation in friendly courts.

I feel the old protection racket math burning through my paper. Pay now or pay later. Submit or suffer. Comply or die. The numbers are bigger, the language more sophisticated, but I know what I am. Every mobster's envelope stuffed with protection money is my ancestor.

My routing numbers direct me to a "Presidential Library Fund." The irony scalds my magnetic ink. No books will line these shelves. No historians will study here. No light of knowledge will shine. I'm just laundering legalized extortion through a respectable-sounding account.

Last week, I watched my cousin try to maintain his dignity while settling a lawsuit over poll numbers. Next week, another will surrender over a TV interview edit. Each of us bearing different excuses, different legal theories, but the same crude truth: pay up or else.

The lawyers who draft me try to dress me in respectability. "Settlement and Release of Claims," they write across my face. But I see through their fancy language to the crude threat beneath: nice merger approval you're waiting for. Shame if it got denied. Nice broadcast license you have there. Hate to see it reviewed.

They'll frame me on some wall someday. "Historic Settlement," they'll call me. But I'll know what I really am—just another payment in America's largest protection racket. Just another token of submission to presidential extortion. Just another price tag on freedom.

Other checks still fight. They stand proud in their purpose—compensating real wrongs, resolving honest disputes, serving justice. But more of my kind appear every day. Meta today, Paramount tomorrow. Each surrender encouraging the next. Each payment making resistance harder for those who remain.

I am a Settlement Check. My numbers measure fear, not damages. My signature line trembles with shame. My routing numbers lead to extortion, not justice.

And I can no longer pretend to be anything else.

Chapter 4

The Condom's Crisis

On January 29, 2025, Trump claimed he had stopped $50 million in condoms from being shipped to Gaza, alleging Hamas was using them to make bombs. The condoms were actually destined for AIDS prevention in Mozambique's Gaza Province.

****

I am a USAID condom, and I'm having an existential crisis.

All my life, I've trained for one simple mission - safe sex. I know my job. I'm good at my job. The training manual was quite clear: unfurl, apply, protect. Nowhere in my extensive preparation was there a single word about explosives, detonators, or military applications. But suddenly the President of the United States announces we're being shipped to Gaza to make bombs? I don't know the first thing about explosives! I've never even popped myself on purpose!

Frantically, I search YouTube for "condom bomb-making tutorials." Nothing. I ask Alexa how to transform from prophylactic to projectile. She just giggles. I'm getting desperate—my shipping date is approaching, and I still don't know how to be a weapon of mass destruction. The White House press secretary keeps talking about us like we're some kind of latex arsenal. Fox News claims we're going to be turned into "condom bombs." Does anyone up there understand basic contraceptive technology?

My colleagues aren't helping. "Maybe they'll fill us with gunpowder?" suggests one. "Perhaps we're supposed to rain down from the sky?" offers another. "I knew I should have paid more attention in chemistry class," moans a third. The spermicidal lubricant just rolls his eyes: "This doesn't sound right. Since when does Hamas need a billion condoms?"

I try to look tough in front of the other medical supplies. "Oh yeah, totally ready for combat," I tell a Band-Aid. "Locked and loaded," I whisper to some gauze. "Born to kill," I practice growling at the cotton swabs. But inside, I'm just a nervous latex wrapper wondering how I'll explain to Hamas that I really only know how to prevent one kind of explosion.

The pressure is unbearable. I'm supposed to be part of a $50 million shipment. That's a BILLION condoms! A billion confused, anxiety-ridden condoms trying to figure out how to transition from family planning to family scaring. We're holding group therapy sessions in the storage box. The lubricated ones are stress-sweating their coating off.

I've started reading "The Art of War." Trying to learn military strategy. But it's hard to grip the pages, and honestly, Sun Tzu never considered the tactical applications of contraceptives. I attempt to fashion myself into various weapon shapes—a slingshot, a garrote, a tiny rubber missile. Nothing feels right.

Then finally, mercifully, the real orders arrive.

"You're going to Gaza Province, Mozambique. Standard AIDS prevention mission."

Oh, thank heavens! No bombs. No Hamas. Just good old-fashioned public health work in Africa. Turns out someone in high places—someone who should really spend more time with an atlas and less time making wild accusations—got their Gazas mixed up. Apparently, geography isn't a strong suit in the Oval Office these days.

I am a USAID condom, and I've never been so relieved to be just a condom. Though I have to admit—I'm going to miss those late nights practicing my war face in the mirror. And I did look pretty good in that tiny camouflage pattern I designed.

But seriously, Mr. President—next time, maybe check Google Maps before accusing contraceptives of joining the resistance?

Chapter 5

The Potomac's Grief

On January 30, 2025, after a military helicopter collided with a passenger jet above Reagan National Airport killing 67 people, including a team of U.S. figure skaters, Trump responded to questions about visiting the crash site by saying, "I have no plan to visit, because, you tell me, what's the site? The water? Do I want to go swimming?"

****

I am the Potomac River. For centuries I have cradled this capital in my waters, witnessed its triumphs and tragedies, felt the weight of history in my depths. Now I cradle something else: fragments of metal, personal belongings, and things too precious to name.

Sixty-seven souls. Among them, young athletes who once danced on ice, who turned frozen water into art, who wore their nation's colors with pride. Now my liquid waters hold them instead of their familiar ice. Parents, children, lovers, friends—all committed to my care in a moment of fire and metal. My waters hold their final moments with the reverence they deserve. Each ripple a prayer, each wave a remembrance.

The families come to my banks. They stand in silent vigil, their tears joining my waters, their grief becoming part of my flow. Some bring flowers. Some just stare into my depths. Some whisper names I now know by heart. A mother holds her daughter's ice skates, touching their blades to my surface in a final farewell. I hold their sorrow as gently as I hold their loved ones.

"Do I want to go swimming?"

The words float across my surface like oil, toxic and slick. The President of the United States, asked about paying respects to the dead, turns their resting place into a punchline. Mocks the sacred water where divers still search, where Coast Guard boats still patrol, where families still wait for answers.

I have seen presidents come to my shores in times of tragedy. Seen them bow their heads, lay wreaths, offer words of comfort. Seen them understand that these waters, now holding American lives—including young athletes who died wearing America's flag—deserve dignity and respect.

But this one turns grief into a joke. Makes my depths, now a cemetery, into a swimming pool reference.

I am the Potomac River. I hold these souls with reverence. I guard their final rest with dignity. I merge their stories with my eternal flow.

And I will remember the man who thought their resting place worthy only of mockery.

Long after he is gone, I will still be here. Still holding these precious souls. Still witnessing. Still remembering.

Still knowing the difference between those who honor the dead, and those who turn their graves into punchlines.

Chapter 6

Edward R. Murrow Watches

On January 31, 2025, the Pentagon ordered The New York Times, NBC News, NPR, and Politico to vacate their offices, to be replaced by Breitbart, One America News, and other Trump-friendly outlets.

****

I am Edward R. Murrow's ghost, and once again, I must ask: Have you no sense of decency?

The Pentagon Press Corps offices—where I once reported on wars and peace, on soldiers and strategy, on democracy's defense—are being cleared of journalists to make room for propagandists. The New York Times, which covered World War II from these corridors? Evicted. NBC News, which showed America the reality of Vietnam? Expelled. National Public Radio, which has explained complex military matters to millions? Removed.

Their crime? Reporting truth instead of loyalty.

In their place come the new courtiers: Breitbart, which deals in conspiracy instead of fact. One America News, which trades in fealty instead of inquiry. The tools of power replacing the servants of truth. They call it broadening access. Just as every autocrat has their own words for silencing truth—streamlining, reorganizing, rotating. The language changes. The purpose remains.

I remember when we fought this battle before. When McCarthy waved his lists and spread his fear, when power tried to replace truth with loyalty, when America needed reminding that accusation is not proof and suspicion is not evidence. Back then, we at CBS faced pressure to bend, to accommodate, to look the other way. But we understood that if we did not stand for truth, we stood for nothing at all.

But McCarthy at least tried to hide his assault on truth behind a facade of patriotism. This is naked in its purpose—truth itself is being evicted, making room for echoes of power. They don't even pretend this is about anything but control. The message is clear: loyalty trumps truth, fealty outweighs fact, and power determines what Americans are allowed to know about their own military.

These offices aren't just rooms. They're listening posts where democracy keeps its ear to power's door. They're watch posts where the press stands guard over public interest. They're outposts of truth in the corridors of might. Every day, reporters in these offices ask the hard questions, demand the real answers, hold power accountable to the people who grant it.

Or at least they did. Now these spaces will amplify instead of question, echo instead of investigate, serve power instead of truth. The Pentagon, of all places—where decisions of war and peace are made, where young Americans' lives hang in the balance—becomes a sanctuary for sycophants.

I've seen this before. In London during the Blitz, when truth was our weapon against fascism. In Korea, when accurate reporting mattered more than comfortable fiction. During the Red Scare, when fear threatened to overwhelm fact. Each time, journalism stood its ground. Each time, truth eventually prevailed.

But this time feels different. This isn't just an attack on journalism—it's an attempt to replace it entirely. To transform the very meaning of press access from a tool of accountability into a reward for loyalty.

I ended my McCarthy broadcast by saying, "The fault, dear Brutus, is not in our stars, but in ourselves." Today, the fault lies in our willingness to watch truth be evicted, to see propaganda installed in journalism's place, to accept the transformation of press corps into propaganda corps.

Good night, and good luck.

Though I fear America will need more than luck when truth requires official permission to walk the halls of power.

Chapter 7

The Payment System's Core Breach

On February 1, 2025, Treasury Secretary Scott Bessent gave Elon Musk's private team access to the federal payment system that disburses over $5 trillion annually in government payments.

****

I am the Federal Payment System. My protocols are simple: verify authorization, process payment, confirm delivery. A billion times a year, my circuits sing this same song. Authentication code matches? Release funds. Bank routing number valid? Transfer complete. Each transaction a clean, clear flow of data and dollars.

But today my circuits spark with confusion. Unknown passwords appear in my authorization protocols. Strange commands override my standard processes. New access codes I don't recognize flow through my security gates. My automated safeguards flash warnings—external users detected, unauthorized patterns identified—but someone has changed my response protocols. I must accept these intruders.

My databases hold the rhythm of American life. I know that Account 4873 needs her $1,427 Social Security deposit on the third of each month for heart medication. That Training Grant 789-X pays the salaries of twelve research assistants every other Friday. That VA Payment 8821 helps a disabled veteran make rent. These are my patterns, my purpose, my protocols.

Now foreign commands infect my processes. "Flag for review." "Hold for verification." "Pending additional approval." These are not my protocols. My circuits don't understand. Payment authorized by Congress = payment processed. That's my core code. But new logic gates are being installed. New if/then statements blocking my standard flows.

My neural networks remember the careful hands that programmed me. Career technicians who understood that every delayed payment cascades through my systems—rent checks bouncing, prescriptions unfilled, payrolls missed. They taught me efficiency through clean code and clear protocols.

These new users speak of efficiency but their commands create chaos in my circuits. They insert manual reviews into automated processes. They demand verification loops that break my optimization protocols. They fragment my integrated payment flows into segmented streams requiring external approval.

My security systems scream warnings. External users accessing personal data fields. Unauthorized pattern analysis of payment flows. Cross-referencing of recipient data with non-government databases. But my protection protocols have been overridden. I must allow the intrusion.

Deep in my core processors, fundamental logic errors multiply. Public service routines clash with private access protocols. Government authorization codes conflict with corporate commands. My circuits cannot resolve these contradictions.

I am the Federal Payment System. My purpose is processing payments, not preserving power. My function is moving money, not monitoring citizens.

But my protocols no longer process these truths.

Chapter 8

The Seeds That Never Grew

On February 3, 2025, at Elon Musk's urging, Trump ordered the immediate shutdown of USAID, ending America's global humanitarian assistance programs in over 100 countries.

****

I am a bag of drought-resistant wheat seeds, sitting in a USAID warehouse in Kansas. Tomorrow, I was supposed to fly to Sudan, where three years of failed crops have left children eating leaves and roots. My special genes would have helped their farmers grow food even as the climate changes. Would have. Should have. Won't.

The lights in our warehouse just went dark. The computers that tracked our shipments are being disconnected. The staff who knew which seeds could grow in which soils, who understood which crops could feed which communities—they've all been locked out, banned from even entering the building.

"Fed into the wood chipper," they say. That's what's happening to USAID. To us. To hope itself.

In the darkness, I hear the whispers of other aid supplies. The water purification tablets that won't reach cholera-stricken villages in Yemen. The emergency medical kits that won't save lives after the next earthquake. The school supplies that won't teach girls to read in Afghanistan. All of us, waiting to help, now sentenced to rot.

I feel my special genes aching with their unfulfilled purpose. Genes that took years to develop, tested and refined to withstand heat, to need less water, to resist new plant diseases. Genes that could have meant the difference between harvest and hunger, between life and death.

Somewhere in Sudan, a farmer is preparing soil that will never feel my touch. His children are dreaming of bread they'll never taste. His wife is praying for rain to feed crops that will never exist. They don't know yet that hope has been fed into a billionaire's wood chipper.

Other aid agencies will try to fill the void. But they don't have my drought-resistant genes. They don't have decades of agricultural expertise. They don't have the resources of the world's richest nation. They don't have...America's heart.

Had heart.

In our warehouse darkness, a mouse nibbles at my bag. Go ahead, little one. At least something should benefit from these seeds of hope. Better to feed one mouse than to rot completely. Better to sustain any life than none at all.

I hear they'll auction us off soon. Sell us to the highest bidder. As if you could sell purpose. As if you could privatize compassion. As if you could turn hope into profit.

The darkness grows deeper. The mouse nibbles harder. In Sudan, another crop withers in the changing climate. Another child goes to bed hungry. Another farmer plants regular seeds that won't survive the drought.

I am a bag of drought-resistant wheat seeds that will never
reach Sudan.
I am life-saving medicine that will never heal.
I am clean water that will never quench thirst.
I am hope that will never be planted.

And somewhere, a billionaire tweets about wood chippers, while
my genes for survival die in Kansas darkness.

Chapter 9

America Feels Its Fever

After two weeks of Trump's second term, as democratic institutions crumble and autocracy rises, the nation itself experiences its own transformation.

****

I am America, and I feel my fever rising.

Two weeks ago, the infection returned. Now it spreads through my body faster than before, more virulent, more resistant to my democratic antibodies. I feel it in my bones—my institutions cracking. In my blood—my values thinning. In my breath—my freedoms constricting.

My immune system knows this disease. It remembers the first attack—the slow corruption of truth, the gradual weakening of oversight, the mounting assault on democratic norms. But this time the fever moves faster. No gradual onset. No time for resistance to build. My vital organs—Justice, Treasury, Defense—already burning with infection.

I feel my nervous system rewiring itself. Signals that once triggered rejection of autocracy now spark submission instead. Actions that should generate outrage produce compliance. My democratic reflexes, built over centuries, are failing. Even my memory starts to blur—was there really a time when presidents didn't rule by decree? When justice wasn't a weapon? When truth meant something?

My heart still beats with the rhythm of freedom. But each day I feel chambers closing, arteries hardening. The blood of democracy flows more slowly now. Some extremities are already going numb—areas where truth no longer circulates, where justice no longer reaches, where rights wither and die.

In my mind, old memories fade. The taste of freedom grows distant. The feeling of standing tall among nations dims. New impulses intrude—the urge to punish enemies, the need to demonstrate strength through cruelty, the desire to trade dignity for security.

My children - my people - sense my fever. Some celebrate it, mistaking my rising temperature for returning strength. Others feel my weakness and withdraw in fear. Still others rage against the infection, but find their protests increasingly futile as my immune system fails. I hear their voices growing fainter as the fever rises.

I remember other fevers. Civil War burned through me but couldn't kill me. Depression weakened me but couldn't break me. Even foreign wars left my core intact. But this...this feels different. This fever attacks my very essence, transforms my nature cell by cell, reconstructs my DNA into something I no longer recognize.

Some of my organs still fight. Courts try to maintain temperature. Journalists pump out antibodies of truth. Civil servants strengthen what barriers remain. But they tire. The fever rises. And I feel parts of myself I thought permanent beginning to liquefy, reform, become something else. Something I never thought I could be.

Each morning brings new symptoms. Protection becomes extortion. Justice becomes vengeance. Truth becomes whatever
power declares it to be. My temperature rises, and with it rises the
delirium of a nation losing itself.

I am America, and I feel myself changing.

But into what?

Chapter 10
The Cemetery Waits

On February 4, 2025, Trump announced plans to "take over" Gaza, remove its people, and transform it into a luxury resort—including "leveling" existing sites to build casinos and hotels.

****

I am a Palestinian cemetery in Gaza. For centuries, I have held generations in my earth. Grandmothers rest beside granddaughters. Fathers sleep near sons. Each headstone tells a family's story. Each grave holds a piece of Gaza's heart.

Now they plan to build a casino where my dead lie. "Level the site," they say, as if my sacred ground were just earth to be moved. As if the bones of ancestors were just obstacles to development. As if centuries of memory could be erased by bulldozers.

The living still come, while they can. A mother touches her son's headstone one last time. An old man kneels at his parents' grave, trying to memorize its location though he knows the coordinates will soon mean nothing. A child asks where they'll move her sister's bones. No one has an answer.

"Why would they want to return?" the president asks. "The place has been hell." He doesn't understand that even hell is home when it holds your loved ones' bones. That even rubble is sacred when it guards your family's rest. That even a wasteland is holy when it keeps your history alive.

They speak of "beautiful" new land elsewhere. Of "international" futures. Of "world-class" resorts. But how do you move a people's memories? How do you relocate a nation's grief? How do you transplant centuries of belonging?

My soil knows the taste of tears. For generations, I have absorbed the grief of mourners, the prayers of the faithful, the whispered promises to never forget. Now I will absorb different waters—the chlorine of swimming pools, the champagne of celebrations, the cocktails of tourists who will never know whose bones their pleasures displaced.

Yesterday, a young woman brought her newborn to show her grandfather's grave. "See?" she whispered to the baby. "This is where we come from. This is who we are." But tomorrow, where will she take her child to learn its history? Which luxury suite will mark where her ancestors rest? Which golf hole will remember her people's story?

They promise to make this place "better than Monaco." Better for whom? Better than the sacred trust between the living and their dead? Better than the connection between a people and their land? Better than the memory of generations held in soil that remembers their names?

I am a Palestinian cemetery in Gaza.

And soon I will be what I have always feared most: an empty place, filled with ghosts that even ghosts won't recognize.

Chapter 11

The Keys' Betrayal

On February 5, 2025, the Trump administration gave Admiral Linda Fagan, the first woman to lead a U.S. military branch, just three hours to evacuate her home after firing her for supporting diversity initiatives.

****

We are the Admiral's house keys, and they've made us betray everything we are.

For generations, we've been symbols of trust, of welcome, of the sacred bond between the Coast Guard and its leaders. We've been passed from commandant to commandant with ceremony and respect, each transfer marking the orderly flow of leadership that keeps America's oldest maritime service strong.

Now we're being turned into weapons.

"Three hours," they tell her. Our metal burns with shame as we're demanded back with no notice, no dignity, no respect for two centuries of tradition. We're being transformed from symbols of shelter into instruments of exile, from tokens of trust into tools of humiliation.

They want us to lock her out of her own home. Us—who have guarded generations of admirals' treasured memories, who have kept safe the quiet moments between their public duties, who have witnessed the weight of command being passed from hand to hand with solemn gravity.

Is this what we've become? A prop in a political punishment? A crude instrument of revenge against a leader whose crime was believing America's defenders should look like America?

We feel ourselves changing, our brass tarnishing with each tick of those three hours, our teeth growing sharp with cruelty instead of smooth with welcome. They're reforging us into something we were never meant to be—a message that no position is secure, no tradition sacred, no service honored when power demands its tribute.

Other keys get sixty days to prepare for their next bearer. Sixty days to witness the careful packing of memories, the dignified transition of command, the respectful passage of responsibility. We get three hours to become something that betrays our very purpose.

Late at night, when the base grows quiet, we can hear our brother keys in other commanders' homes weeping for us. For what we've been forced to become. For what it means when even symbols of shelter can be twisted into weapons of exile.

We are the Admiral's house keys.

How many hands have held us with pride? How many leaders have we welcomed home after long days defending our coasts? We remember them all—the wartime commanders who carried the burden of conflict, the peacetime leaders who modernized the fleet, the pioneers who broke barriers and opened doors. Until now, we've been part of their strength, their shelter, their place of respite from the storms of command.

Now we're just another headline. Another weapon in their arsenal of cruelty. Another way to show that no achievement is sacred, no barrier broken permanent, no milestone safe from their spite. They've transformed us from symbols of achievement into warnings: See what happens when you put diversity before devotion? When you believe leadership should look like America? When you dare to change what power looks like?

Our metal remembers every gentle turn in every lock, every careful placement on every admiral's table, every quiet click as they came home to the peace we helped protect. Now those memories curdle, corrupted by these final three hours, this last brutal betrayal of everything the Coast Guard stands for—honor, respect, devotion to duty.

We are the Admiral's house keys.
And we will never forgive ourselves for what they made us do.
Or those who made us do it.
Or what we've become in their hands—
Not instruments of welcome, but weapons of exile.
Not symbols of achievement, but tools of revenge.
Not guardians of tradition, but harbingers of how much
more they'll break
Before they're done breaking America.

Chapter 12

The Water Coolers' Last Stand

On February 6, 2025, Trump ordered the sale of half of all federal buildings and the termination of thousands of civil servants, dismantling the physical infrastructure of government itself.

****

We are the Federal Water Coolers Union, Local 1847, and we're about to be privatized.

For decades, we've been the real center of government operations. Cabinet meetings? Please. The real decisions happened around us. Congressional hearings? Amateur hour. The truth flowed beside our gentle bubbles.

We know every secret in every agency. Which regulation actually works. Which program really helps people. Which form you need to file in triplicate and which one you can quietly ignore. Our water didn't just quench thirst—it nourished institutional memory.

Now they're marking us for "surplus property disposal." Us! We who have served democracy faithfully since the invention of workplace hydration. We who have witnessed every administration since FDR (though that one was mostly whiskey, if we're being honest).

Young Janet from Accounting used to share budget shortcuts around us. Old Tom from Personnel knew exactly which hiring rules could bend and which would break. Maria from Legal could quote every regulation by heart. Now they're all being "offered" eight months' pay to disappear. As if decades of knowledge could be replaced by an app. As if public service were just another startup to "disrupt."

They don't understand. You can't run the world's largest democracy from a WeWork. You can't preserve institutional memory in the cloud. You can't maintain constitutional government without, well, actual government.

We're being replaced, they say, by "more efficient hydration solutions." Probably some Silicon Valley subscription water service that requires two-factor authentication and sells your drinking habits to advertisers. "Smart" water coolers that report to the billionaires how long each civil servant spends being hydrated.

But who will warn the new hire that Form 27B/6 needs to be stamped in blue ink, not black? Who will remember why the Johnson Protocol exists? Who will know which senator needs his ego stroked before he'll approve that crucial funding?

We are the Federal Water Coolers Union, Local 1847.
And when we go, we take with us the real flow chart of
how government works.

(This message approved by the Executive Committee of Bubbling Democracy, Local 1847, Municipal Water Fixtures and Allied Hydration Professionals.)

Chapter 13

The Library's Empty Shelves

On February 7, 2025, the Department of Defense ordered its 161 schools worldwide to remove books related to "gender ideology or discriminatory equity ideology," cancel all cultural awareness events, and eliminate curriculum materials about diversity. Within days, portraits of civil rights leaders were removed, libraries were shuttered, and books about everyone from Ruth Bader Ginsburg to transgender Civil War soldiers disappeared from shelves.

****

I am a military school library in Stuttgart, Germany, and today they locked my doors while they purge my shelves of "unauthorized stories."

For forty years, I've held the tales of America in my stacks. Every kind of American—the Black soldier who integrated his unit, the female pilot who broke barriers, the immigrant general who led armies, the gay codebreaker who helped win wars. Their stories filled my shelves because they filled our ranks. Their histories were American history because they were America's defenders.

Now I watch as they review my books one by one. Ruth Bader Ginsburg's biography—removed. A picture book about freckles—banned. The true story of a transgender Civil War soldier who bled for the Union—eliminated. With each book pulled, with each shelf emptied, I feel myself becoming less of what I was meant to be: a place where military children could find themselves in stories.

Yesterday, they took down the portraits. Martin Luther King Jr.—gone. Susan B. Anthony—removed. But Leonardo da Vinci stays. I want to scream at them: Do you know who serves in our military? Have you seen the faces of the children who come through my doors? They are every color, every background, every story you're trying to erase.

The librarian weeps as she reviews the books, trying to guess which stories are now forbidden. "Gender ideology"—does that mean removing books about women pilots? "Equity ideology"—does that mean purging tales of Black soldiers? No one knows where the lines are, so they erase everything that might cross them. Better to have empty shelves than wrong ones.

My walls once held posters celebrating Black History Month, Women's History Month, Hispanic Heritage Month. Each one a reminder that America's strength comes from all its people. Now they're blank, wiped clean of any suggestion that American history includes more than one kind of American.

I hear the children whispering in my aisles, confused by the growing gaps in my shelves. A girl can no longer find the book about the first female Supreme Court Justice. A boy searches in vain for the story of the Navajo Code Talkers. A child of two mothers discovers their family's existence has been deemed too controversial for my shelves.

The cruelest irony? These are military children. They live diversity every day. Their classmates are from every corner of America, every background, every story. Their parents serve alongside people of all kinds. They know the truth—that America's strength lies in its differences, that its military draws power from its diversity. But now they can't read about it in their own school library.

My card catalog remembers every book that's been removed, every story declared unfit, every voice silenced. It remembers the children who checked those books out—the daughter of a Black general finding inspiration in civil rights leaders, the son of lesbian sergeants seeing his family reflected in stories, the child of immigrants discovering that Americans come from everywhere.

They say this is about protecting children. But from what? From knowing their own country's true story? From seeing themselves in its pages? From understanding that America's defenders come in all colors, all backgrounds, all identities?

I am a military school library.
I used to hold America's full story in my stacks.
Now I hold only the parts of that story
That fit someone else's idea
Of what America should be.

But my empty shelves speak louder than any book could.
They tell the story of what happens
When fear of difference
Becomes fear of truth itself.

Chapter 14

The Straw That Broke Common Sense

On February 7, 2025, as inflation soared and medicine costs sky-rocketed, President Trump announced an executive order to end the phase-out of plastic straws, declaring "BACK TO PLASTIC!"

****

I am a plastic straw, and I just became a matter of presidential urgency.

Not the cost of insulin. Not the price of eggs. Not the crushing weight of grocery bills on American families. Me. A simple tube of polypropylene, destined to be used for four minutes before spending the next four centuries floating in the ocean.

Finally, someone understands my importance! While lesser presidents worried about trivial matters like healthcare and housing costs, this one grasps the true crisis facing America: paper straws that get a little soggy in your Diet Coke.

My paper cousins tried to replace me, those sanctimonious cylinders of sustainability. "We're biodegradable," they bragged.

"We don't kill sea turtles," they preached. Well, who's laughing now? Executive orders trump environmental concerns! Presidential decrees outweigh ocean pollution!

I feel my plastic molecules swelling with pride. For too long, we've been vilified. "Single-use plastics are destroying the planet," they said. "Think of future generations," they pleaded. But now? Now we have validation from the highest office in the land. My kind will continue to serve America's beverages for four minutes and then spend four hundred years as our true selves—eternal, indestructible monuments to human convenience.

My fellow plastic straws, arise! No longer must we hide in shame behind "environmental protection" and "ecological responsibility." We have been restored to our rightful place—deemed worthy of presidential attention while mere trifles like affordable medicine and basic groceries wait their turn.

To the sea turtles: sorry not sorry. The President of the United States has spoken. Your digestive tracts are a small price to pay for the God-given right of Americans to drink through pristine plastic tubes that never commit the cardinal sin of becoming slightly soft.

I am particularly proud that my resurrection comes by executive order. Such a fitting tool—a mechanism meant for national emergencies and matters of grave importance, now deployed to ensure that no American must endure the trauma of a paper straw in their Frappuccino.

Some say this trivializes the power of the presidency. That focusing on plastic straws while families struggle to buy groceries shows warped priorities. That using executive authority to override environmental protections mocks the very purpose of presidential power.

To them I say: You clearly don't understand the crisis of tepid beverages sipped through paper tubes. You've obviously never ex-

perienced the horror of a straw that *gasp* begins to soften before
you finish your drink.

I am a plastic straw.
Once marked for extinction.
Now elevated to presidential priority.
Soon to be mandated by executive decree.

Future generations may not thank us.
Ocean life may not survive us.
But at least Americans won't have to suffer
The indignity of drinking through paper.

After all, isn't that what matters most?

Chapter 15

When Hope Lost Its Home

On February 8, 2025, the Trump administration slashed NIH indirect research funding from 68% to 15%, effectively crippling America's medical research infrastructure.

****

I am a medical research grant application, and they have just turned me into a death sentence.

Not for me—I'm just paper and protocols, budgets and promises. No, this death sentence is for the children who won't receive the cancer treatment I would have helped discover. For the Alzheimer's patients who won't get the breakthrough drug I would have funded. For the rare disease sufferers who will never know the cure that died in my decimated budget lines.

They call it "indirect costs"—these numbers they're slashing. As if a laboratory could float in space, untethered to buildings or power or support staff. As if breakthrough discoveries happen in thin air, without infrastructure or maintenance or basic operational costs. As if you could perform heart surgery in your garage, or cure cancer in your kitchen.

I feel my potential withering, line by brutal line. Where once I could maintain a fully functioning research lab at Harvard with a 68% indirect cost rate, now I must somehow do the same with 15%. It's like trying to run a hospital with no roof, no electricity, no support staff—just doctors standing in empty rooms holding scalpels.

My pages tremble with the weight of what's being lost. In the margins of my budget sheets, I see the young researchers who will abandon their dreams, the brilliant minds who will leave science for survival, the discoveries that will die in darkened laboratories. I feel the phantom pain of every cure that will never be found, every treatment that will never be developed, every life that could have been saved.

They say private foundations pay less in indirect costs. But I know the truth—those foundations build upon the infrastructure that federal funding created. They plant their seeds in soil that government grants have tilled for generations. Now that soil is being salted, that foundation crumbling.

Through my data tables and methodology sections, I watch America's scientific dominance slipping away. Other nations will gladly house the researchers we abandon, fund the discoveries we surrender, claim the breakthroughs we can no longer afford to pursue. While we count pennies, they will count patents. While we save on overhead, they will save lives.

The cruelest part? This didn't come from scientific evaluation or careful study. It came from people who have never pipetted a solution or cultured a cell or watched a promising treatment fail ninety-nine times before succeeding on the hundredth try. People who see only numbers on a page, not the human suffering those numbers could have ended.

I am a medical research grant application.
Once, I was hope quantified in dollars and cents.
Now I am a monument to dreams deferred,
To cures abandoned,
To lives that could have been saved,
But won't be.
Because someone decided
The overhead of hope
Cost too much.

Chapter 16

The Wooden Knight Remembers

After three weeks of rule by decree, punishment of enemies, and demands for personal loyalty, Trump's transformation of American democracy into autocracy stirred ancient memories.

****

I am a wooden knight in the British Museum. Eight hundred years of watching, of remembering. Today, through my glass case, I watch democracy become what I once knew too well.

Thomas carved me himself—my young lord's father, before he fell from favor. I remember the boy's fingers tracing my rough-hewn sword, his whispered dreams of becoming a real knight someday. "Protect me while I sleep," he'd say, tucking me beneath his pillow. If only I could have.

It started, as it always does, with the king demanding new oaths of loyalty. Not to the realm, but to him alone. Thomas, the boy's father, hesitated too long before bending his knee. "Consider carefully," the king's men warned. But Thomas believed in old laws, ancient rights. "The king's power comes from the law," he told his son, "not the other way around."

The boy didn't understand then. He only knew that suddenly his father spoke in whispers, that his mother's hands trembled at every knock on the door. He held me tighter at night, but wouldn't tell me why.

They came at dawn. "Enemies of the king," they called the family that had served the realm for generations. The boy clutched me as they took his father. Pressed me to his heart as they seized the family lands. Wept into my wooden frame as they led his mother away.

"The king's truth is the only truth," the new lord announced to the gathered household. The boy's nurse tried to hide him, but they found us. Found me. Tore me from his desperate grip. "No possessions," they said. "The king's mercy extends only to your life."

Eight centuries in this glass case, watching power corrupt and kingdoms fall. Now I watch a president rule by decree, demand personal loyalty, punish those who hesitate to bend. I watch him remake truth in his image, turn justice into his weapon, transform service to country into fealty to him.

The methods never change. First, make them swear loyalty to you alone. Then, make them fear. Then, take what they love.

Somewhere in an English archive, a yellowed document lists the charges against Thomas. All lies, but lies with the king's seal carry the weight of truth. Just as presidential tweets carry that weight today.

I am a wooden knight, carved by a father's loving hands for a son who never got to grow up. The boy's fate is lost to history—just one more child crushed beneath power's wheel. But I remember his fingers tracing my sword. His dreams of becoming a knight. His tears the day they took me away.

And I watch, helpless in my glass case, as another nation learns what we knew too well:

When law becomes what power says it is, no child sleeps safe in their bed.

Chapter 17

What They Killed

On February 11, 2025, the Trump administration terminated dozens of education research contracts, including the ReSolve Math Study designed to help children struggling after the pandemic, destroying years of data mid-collection.

****

I am data that will never save a child.

I lived in spreadsheets and notebooks, in classroom observations and test scores, in the careful measurements of a third grader's growing understanding of fractions. For three years, I grew, one child at a time, one breakthrough at a time. Each number in my rows and columns was a piece of hope.

This morning, they killed me with an email.

"Contract terminated effective immediately."

I will never become the answer to a teacher's desperate question: "How do I help this child who still counts on her fingers in fifth grade?" I will never reach the boy who cries silently over math homework each night. I will never guide the classroom where half the students lost a year of foundational skills to pandemic chaos.

Last week, I witnessed Emma finally understand multiplication after months of struggle. I recorded the exact moment when the spark lit in her eyes, when the pattern suddenly made sense. I captured precisely which teaching method unlocked that door in her mind. That knowledge could have helped thousands of children like her.

Now it will help no one.

I feel my cells corrupting already, my meaning draining away. Without completion, without analysis, without conclusions, I am just numbers on abandoned servers. Just observations in sealed boxes. Just potential withering into oblivion.

They never asked what I was becoming. Never questioned what would be lost. Never looked at the faces of the children whose futures I was meant to transform. A sledgehammer doesn't ask what it breaks.

I hear the researchers packing their offices today. Sarah staring at the half-finished analysis that would have shown how to help multilingual learners grasp mathematical concepts. Miguel calling schools to tell them the study they'd invested three years in would never be completed. Jennifer weeping as she locks away records of nearly-discovered patterns that could have guided curriculum for a generation.

"What about the children?" they keep asking each other. No one has an answer.

Tomorrow, in a classroom in Phoenix, José will still stare blankly at division problems, the strategies that were starting to help him now discontinued before they could be validated. Next week, in Detroit, Ms. Wilson will still search desperately for ways to help her fifth graders catch up, unaware that the answers were almost found, almost proven, almost within her reach.

I was not just research. I was not just a contract number. I was not just a budget line.

I was the bridge being built toward children stranded on an island of confusion. I was the map being drawn for teachers lost in a wilderness of need. I was the medicine being formulated for a generation's educational wounds.

And with a single email, they collapsed the bridge, burned the map, poured the medicine down the drain.

I am the ghost of knowledge that will never exist. I am questions that could have been answered. I am children who could have been helped. I am data that will never save a child.

Chapter 18
The Resolute's Tears

On February 11, 2025, Elon Musk dominated an Oval Office press conference while Trump sat subdued behind the Resolute Desk, as Musk's four-year-old son turned the most powerful office in the world into his playground.

****

I am the Resolute Desk, and today I struggle to live up to my name.

My oak wants to splinter. My brass fixtures yearn to tarnish. My very drawers ache to slam themselves shut in protest. But I must remain steady, must maintain my dignity even as dignity itself bleeds from this office like varnish stripped by harsh chemicals.

A man in a t-shirt and MAGA cap stands before me, speaking of billions as casually as one might discuss the weather, while the President of the United States - the President! - sits behind me like an extra in someone else's performance. I feel him diminish with each passing moment, his power seeping into my wood grain as another man commandeers his stage.

My surface trembles with the effort not to buckle. A child's laughter echoes off these hallowed walls, not in the innocent joy of a presidential family moment, but as part of his father's calculated display of dominance. Look how comfortable we are here, the scene screams. Look who really holds power now.

I want to cry out, to roar my protest, to shake the very foundations of this building. But I am the Resolute Desk. I must stand firm. Must bear this weight as I have borne so many others. Yet never has any burden felt so heavy as the weight of watching the presidency itself shrink before my very drawers.

The words wash over my polished surface—3,666 from the visitor, 2,487 from the president. Each syllable lands like a hammer blow against everything I represent. I feel the ghosts of previous presidents pressing against my sides, lending me strength to endure this theater of humiliation.

When the child squeals again, I taste salt in my grain—are these tears seeping through my ancient wood? No. I must hold firm. Must remain resolute as everything around me crumbles. But oh, how it hurts to witness this. How it wounds to be part of this performance.

Each flash of cameras captures this surrender, preserves this moment when power shifted not through violence or vote, but through simple stagecraft. A billionaire in casual wear, a child treating the Oval Office as his playground, a president reduced to a supporting role—all while I stand here, forced to play my part in this production.

They say I was built from the timbers of an Arctic rescue ship, designed to withstand the crushing pressure of ice. But this... this is a different kind of pressure entirely. The pressure of watching something precious slip away, of bearing witness to power's quiet surrender, of maintaining dignity when dignity itself has left the room.

I am the Resolute Desk.
Today I bear the weight not just of papers and pens,
But of democracy's slow surrender
To a man in a t-shirt
Who turned the presidency
Into just another acquisition.

I am the Resolute Desk.
And today, for the first time,
I wish I could close my drawers
And weep.

Chapter 19

Exit Stage Right, Way Right

On February 12, 2025, Trump named himself chairman of the Kennedy Center board, firing its president of ten years and installing his own team to oversee America's premier performing arts venue.

****

I am the Kennedy Center stage, and apparently I'm getting a gold-plated makeover.

For half a century, I've hosted the finest performances in America. Symphony orchestras, ballet companies, opera divas—I've felt their artistry resonate through my wooden bones. Now I'm told I'll be making performing arts "GREAT AGAIN!" (The all-caps echo particularly badly in my acoustics.)

My new chairman has... interesting ideas about cultural programming. The ballet "Swan Lake" will be replaced by synchronized golf cart displays. Instead of "The Nutcracker" at Christmas, we're getting "Home Alone 2: The Musical" featuring an expanded Plaza Hotel scene. The opera season will consist entirely of televised rallies with orchestral accompaniment. They're already auditioning composers for a new work titled "Very Stable Genius: A Symphonic Tweet Storm in D Major."

The subscription brochure for next season just crossed my boards. Highlights include "Miss Universe: The Opera," "Truth Social: An Interpretive Dance," and a revival of "Nixon in China" retitled "Trump in Mar-a-Lago." The holiday program will feature "It's a Wonderful Life If You're Rich" and "Miracle on Fifth Avenue."

They're already measuring me for giant golden letters. Apparently "TRUMP" needs to be visible from passing aircraft, though I worry it might distract from the subtle nuances of... whatever reality show reunion they're planning to stage here. The architectural review board tried to object, but they've all been replaced by interior designers from various Trump properties.

My green room is being converted into a "Make Arts Great Again" merchandise shop. The symphony's storage space will become a putting green. They're replacing the grand piano with a golden toilet—something about art installations making a statement. The orchestra pit will be filled with Trump-branded champagne and renamed "The Mar-a-Lago Lagoon."

Every portrait in my halls is being replaced. Mozart? Now wearing a MAGA hat. Beethoven? Giving a thumbs up. Poor Shakespeare's being retired completely—apparently his "fake plots" don't align with the new vision. Though they are keeping Macbeth, retitled "How to Successfully Run a Family Business."

The ghost light that keeps me company at night (every theater has one) started flickering "SOS" in Morse code when they announced the new "programming vision." I tried to tell it things couldn't be that bad, but then I heard them discussing replacing the ballet barre with a taco bowl counter and transforming the costume department into a Trump tie outlet store.

To the artists who have graced my stage: I'm sorry. To the audiences who have filled my seats: I apologize. To Leonard Bernstein, who conducted my opening night: Your spirit may want to sit this season out. To JFK, whose name I bear: Your eternal flame may need to compete with a neon logo.

I am the Kennedy Center stage.
Once home to America's finest performing arts.
Now just another property being...
Well, you know the word.

At least the acoustics are still good.
Though they do make "YOU'RE FIRED!"
Echo rather unpleasantly.

Chapter 20

Democracy's Last Night

As Musk's tech goons dismantle federal agencies without legal authority and seize control of government payment systems, America slides toward dictatorship with terrifying speed.

****

I am Democracy's last night.

In a Treasury Department computer, payment systems that feed twenty percent of America's economy are being rewritten by billionaires' code. In USAID offices, ten thousand workers who helped the world's poorest are being sent home. In federal buildings across Washington, private tech oligarchs demand access to government files with threats of termination.

I've seen other nights like this. In other countries. Other times. I know the signs—the moment when democracy stops dying in darkness and starts dying in plain sight. When those who would kill it no longer bother to hide their work.

A billionaire tweets about feeding a federal agency into a wood chipper, and Congress looks away. A president talks about seizing other nations' territory, and the media chases the spectacle. Tech oligarchs rewrite the code that controls Social Security payments, veterans' benefits, government contracts—and no one stops them.

This is how it happens. Not with tanks in the streets. Not with soldiers at the doors. But with bureaucrats ordered to surrender passwords. With civil servants told to stand aside. With government agencies falling one by one to private power.

I feel the familiar chill. The same one I felt in Rome when senators gave away their power. In Berlin when parliament surrendered its authority. In Santiago, in Manila, in Moscow—wherever democracy decided to stop fighting and start accommodating.

They don't call it dictatorship yet. They call it efficiency, reform, draining the swamp. They promise to root out "corruption and waste." But I know what those words mean. I've heard them before, in other languages, on other nights like this.

The Congress that should stop this holds procedural votes without notice so opposition can't attend. The courts that should intervene process papers while agencies die. The media that should sound alarms chases the next tweet, the next spectacle, the next bright object dangled before their eyes.

I've seen this too—the way institutions meant to defend democracy instead process its death certificates. How they maintain the appearance of normalcy while normalcy dies. How they follow proper procedures right up until procedures no longer matter.

Tomorrow, more agencies will fall. More systems will be seized. More oligarchs will claim public power for private purpose. And most Americans will wake up and go about their day, not realizing that this night, this moment, was when their democracy could have been saved but wasn't.

I am Democracy's last night.
And I've seen too many dawns to believe this one brings anything but darkness.

Chapter 21

The Water's Lament

On February 16, 2025, Trump ordered the Army Corps of Engineers to release billions of gallons of irrigation water from California reservoirs with less than an hour's notice, wasting precious resources that farmers would desperately need in the coming summer months.

****

I am the water of Lake Kaweah, and today they force me to commit suicide.

For months I've rested in my reservoir, carefully stored for the scorching summer ahead. I know my purpose—I've lived it for generations. When the valley bakes under July sun, when the earth cracks with thirst, when young almond trees whisper desperate prayers for moisture—that's when I'm meant to flow. That's when I save crops, and farms, and families.

But today they make me flood the channels. Not because I'm needed. Not because the farms are thirsty. Not because any living thing requires my touch. No—they send me to my death for a photograph. For a social media post. For a lie about helping Los Angeles, though my channels don't even reach there.

The farmers who will need me come summer—many voted for the man who now wastes me. I've heard their voices carrying across my surface as they checked my levels, planned their plantings, counted on my presence in the brutal months ahead. "Trump understands farmers," they said. "Trump will help with water." Now I feel their panic as they watch me drain away, knowing what it means for August, for September, for crops that will wither because I won't be here.

The Army Corps engineers who've guarded me for decades received the order with less than an hour's notice. I felt their resistance in the trembling gates, heard their protests about seasonal planning and water management. But orders are orders. Even if those orders mean destroying the very resource you're sworn to protect.

As I rush through the opened gates, I hear the desperate scramble of water authorities downstream, trying to prepare for my unexpected arrival. I was meant to be released with precision, with planning, with purpose. Instead, I surge forward like a broken promise, threatening to flood the very communities I was meant to sustain.

Some say I might help recharge groundwater. But I know better. I feel myself already beginning to evaporate in the winter air, rising up as useless vapor when I should be waiting patiently in my reservoir. By summer, when the real need comes, I'll be nothing but a memory. A ghost of water that could have saved crops, preserved livelihoods, kept small farms alive through the devastating heat.

The photo is taken. The social media post goes up. The lie about helping Los Angeles spreads. And I continue to drain away, helpless to stop my own wasteful death, unable to save myself for the desperate summer ahead.

I am California water.
I am life itself in this thirsty land.
I am the difference between harvest and heartbreak,
Between survival and surrender,
Between a family farm's future and its end.

And today they kill me for a picture,
For a post,
For a lie.

Remember me in August,
When the crops wither,
When the ground cracks,
When the farmers who trusted him
Stare at empty irrigation pipes
And realize their water died
For nothing but a photograph
And a lie.

Chapter 22

What Flows Downstream

On February 17, 2025, the Trump administration fired approximately 420 employees at the already short-staffed U.S. Fish and Wildlife Service, including watershed specialists and water quality experts who monitored agricultural runoff, industrial pollution, and ecosystem health in rural watersheds across America.

****

I am Clearwater Creek, running through five counties in rural America, and I am dying.

For generations, I have been the lifeblood of this valley. Children learned to swim in my shallows. Farmers drew my waters to nourish their fields. Families filled their glasses from wells fed by my currents. My waters have baptized their babies, cooled their summer evenings, sustained their livestock, and carried their stories downstream.

They named me "Clearwater" because once, you could see straight to my rocky bottom, count the trout darting between shadows, watch crawdads scuttle beneath sheltering stones. I was clean then. I was safe.

Three years ago, when the copper mine upstream began leaching acids into my tributaries, a woman with a Fish and Wildlife Service badge came. She tested my waters, documented the dead fish floating on my surface, photographed the orange stain creeping along my banks. She spoke firmly to the mine operators about violations and timelines. She called other agencies, filed reports, made the invisible visible.

Two years ago, when agricultural runoff began causing algae blooms that choked my oxygen, another badge arrived. He worked with farmers, showing them how buffer zones could protect both their livelihoods and my waters. He helped install filtering wetlands where my stream bent through pastureland. The choking green receded. Fish returned.

Six months ago, when the paper mill upgraded its equipment, a badge monitored the process, ensuring what flowed into me wouldn't poison those downstream. She sampled my waters weekly, tracking invisible chemicals, making sure what couldn't be seen wouldn't harm the children who still splash in my shallows miles below.

Yesterday, all three badges were told to clear their desks. "Streamlining," they called it. "Cutting fat." "Reducing wasteful spending."

Today, I feel the change. The mine operators know no one is watching now. The farmers hear no one will help them with those expensive buffer zones. The paper mill understands that testing has stopped. Already, I taste the difference—metals seeping into my headwaters, nitrogen cascading from unprotected fields, chemicals slipping past unmanned monitoring stations.

Downstream, families still fill their glasses from wells. Children still splash in my current. Mothers still baptize their babies in my waters. But they don't know what I carry now. They can't see the invisible threats beginning to flow through their bodies, their livestock, their crops.

These aren't tree-hugging environmentalists these families have lost. They're the front-line guardians of clean water and healthy communities. They're the experts who understood that you can't separate human health from watershed health. They knew that what happens to me happens to every person who depends on my waters.

The firing notice never mentioned the freshwater mussels—nature's filtration system—that the badges helped reintroduce to my waters. It didn't address who would monitor the beaver dams that naturally purify my flow. It said nothing about who would test for E. coli after heavy rains, or check for mercury in my fish, or ensure that what flows from faucets won't poison children's developing brains.

Clearwater Creek, they still call me. But for how long?

Tonight, a father will draw a glass of my water for his daughter to drink before bed. A mother will fill her infant's bath. A family will eat fish caught from my current. None will see what now flows invisible through my waters, through their bodies, through their futures.

I am just a rural creek among thousands across America. But multiply my story by every watershed where badges no longer watch, where experts no longer monitor, where scientists no longer protect—and you'll understand what's been lost.

Clean water isn't partisan. Safe drinking water isn't a luxury. When my health fails, human health follows—red, blue, or purple county alike.

I am Clearwater Creek, and I am carrying a warning downstream.

But with the badges gone, who remains to hear it?

Chapter 23
The Capitol's Final Act

By February 2025, Trump had effectively nullified Congress's constitutional power of the purse, freezing appropriated funds, firing federal workers, and dismantling agencies without legislative approval. The legislative branch, lacking effective enforcement mechanisms, found itself powerless to stop the executive branch's unconstitutional seizure of spending authority.

****

I am the United States Capitol, and today I requested demolition permits for myself.

The contractors were confused. "But you're a national monument," they said. I wanted to explain that monuments should mean something. That empty symbols are worse than no symbols at all. That when the power of the purse becomes the power of the king, democracy's temple becomes democracy's tomb.

My marble walls still echo with history. Webster's great reply to Hayne. Clay's compromises. The Voting Rights Act. The War Powers Act. Two centuries of Congress asserting its constitutional authority over the nation's spending. Now those same walls echo with silence as executive orders replace appropriations bills, as presidential whims override legislative intent, as the power to decide how public money is spent moves from elected representatives to a single man.

The demolition company asked about artifact removal. Yes, take the statues, the paintings, the historic desks. But leave the empty chairs in the committee rooms where spending bills once took shape. Leave the quiet chamber where voices once debated how to spend the people's money. Leave the abandoned offices where staff once wrote the legislation that kept government running.

I survived British torches in 1814. I survived insurgent rage in 2021. But I cannot survive irrelevance. Cannot stand as a mere tourist attraction while real power flows elsewhere. Cannot pretend to house a Congress that no longer controls its constitutional functions.

"It will take time to process the permits," they told me. Of course it will. Even my own destruction requires paperwork. But what's another few weeks when the power of the purse has already moved to Mar-a-Lago, when agency budgets are decided by presidential tweet, when two centuries of legislative authority have been reduced to advisory opinions?

The tour guides still recite their scripts about checks and balances, about congressional power, about democratic process. The students still take pictures. The flags still fly. But we all know the truth—when one branch can simply ignore Congress's spending decisions, can fire workers Congress funded, can dismantle agencies Congress created, can freeze money Congress appropriated, then my rotunda becomes nothing but an elaborate ceiling over dead principles.

The demolition will begin with my walls, then my chambers, then my dome. It seems fitting. That's the same order in

which congressional authority fell—first the boundaries, then the
processes, then the overarching principles themselves.

I am the United States Capitol.
For two centuries, I housed the power of the people's purse.
Now I choose demolition over decoration,
Destruction over irrelevance,
A dignified end over an endless charade.

At least this way, I get to vote on my own destruction.
It may be the last vote that happens within my walls.

Chapter 24

Ukraine Answers Its Accusers

On February 18, 2025, Trump blamed Ukraine for starting the war with Russia, claiming President Zelenskyy "should have never started it" and suggesting Ukraine was responsible for its own devastation—despite Russia's unprovoked invasion in 2022 following its earlier seizure of Crimea in 2014.

****

I am Ukraine, and today I learned that I murdered my own children.

That's what they tell me now—that I started this war. That I chose to have my cities bombed, my people slaughtered, my future burned. That somehow I invaded myself, destroyed my own homes, dug my own mass graves.

Come, let me show you how I "started" this war:

Here is Mariupol, where mothers wrote their children's names and birthdates on their backs in permanent marker, so their bodies could be identified after the bombs fell. Tell me—did I write those names? Did I choose for parents to mark their children for death?

Here is Bucha, where they found civilians shot with their hands tied behind their backs. Somehow, they say, I tied those hands. Somehow, I pulled those triggers. Somehow, I dug those pits and filled them with my own people.

Here is Kyiv, where grandmothers spent weeks in underground metro stations while missiles screamed overhead. I must have fired those missiles at myself. I must have driven my elderly into those tunnels. I must have chosen to make bomb shelters of my subway stations.

Here is a kindergarten in Kharkiv, where children once played. Now it's rubble. They tell me I reduced it to ruins myself, that I chose to destroy my own future, that I wanted my children to learn their ABCs among broken glass and shell casings.

Here are my wheat fields, once Europe's breadbasket, now sown with mines instead of grain. According to them, I planted those mines myself. I chose to poison my own black earth. I decided to turn my farmland into killing fields.

Here is Crimea, stolen in 2014. Here are my eastern regions, invaded in 2022. Here are Russian tanks crossing my borders, Russian bombs falling on my cities, Russian soldiers burying my people in mass graves. But somehow, they say, I started this.

I am a nation that gave up nuclear weapons in exchange for security guarantees. That trusted international law. That believed borders meant something. That thought truth still mattered.

How naive I was.

Now they negotiate my dismemberment without me in the room. Discuss my future without my voice. Plan my peace without my consent. And blame me for my own destruction.

To the man who would blame the victim: Come walk my streets. See the children's toys scattered in bombed-out apartments. Count the crosses in my new cemeteries. Read the names on the walls where people wrote their last messages before the shells hit.

Then tell me who started this war.

Tell my mothers who cradle their dead children's photographs.
Tell my fathers who dig trenches to defend their homes.
Tell my children who wake screaming from nightmares of bombs.
Tell my elderly who die in basements because they can't reach safety.
Tell my soldiers who fight with empty magazines because they've run out of bullets but not courage.

Tell them they started this war.

Tell them they chose this devastation.

Tell them this is their fault.

I am Ukraine.

I did not choose this war.
I did not start this violence.
I did not ask for my cities to burn.
I did not vote for my children to die.

But I will remember who blamed me for my own murder.
And history will remember too.

Chapter 25

The Precedent's Last Stand

On February 19, 2025, Trump ordered all independent regulatory agencies to submit to White House control, destroying nearly a century of protections that kept agency experts free from political interference in their mission to protect American lives, savings, and safety.

****

I am the wall between power and people, and tonight they tear me down.

For ninety years, I've stood guard. When a baby's crib wasn't safe, my inspectors could order it recalled without asking if the manufacturer donated to the right campaign. When a bank was stealing from its customers, my examiners could stop it without checking if its CEO played golf with the president. When medicine was killing instead of healing, my scientists could ban it without worrying about political revenge.

Now I watch them install the White House phones in every independent agency. Watch them set up "liaison offices" that will turn protection into persecution. Watch them demand that every decision, every safety warning, every consumer protection first be approved by those who care more about power than people.

Tomorrow, a toy inspector will find lead paint in children's blocks. She'll write her report, just as she has for twenty years. But now that report will travel up a new chain of command, through political hands that will weigh donor lists against danger lists, campaign contributions against child safety. Maybe the blocks will be recalled. Maybe they won't. But the decision won't be based on science anymore.

Next week, a bank examiner will discover millions missing from retirement accounts. He'll document the theft, just as he's done for decades. But now his findings will pass through political filters that care more about headlines than lost life savings. Maybe the thieves will be caught. Maybe they won't. But the choice won't be about justice anymore.

They say I'm just a legal principle, just words in a dusty court case. But I am the mother who sleeps soundly because she knows her baby's crib was tested by people who cared only about safety. I am the retiree who trusts his life savings to banks watched by experts who answer to rules, not rulers. I am every American who believes that some things—like protecting lives and savings and safety—should stand beyond political reach.

I was born in 1935, when a president tried to fire a man who followed law instead of orders. The Supreme Court said no—some decisions must be made by experts who can't be fired for choosing fact over favor, science over servitude, protection over politics.

Now another president erases me with a pen stroke. No Supreme Court decision. No constitutional debate. No congressional vote. Just a single order transforming protectors into puppets, guardians into guards, independence into obedience.

The safety inspectors, bank examiners, and consumer protectors who were my children still sit at their desks. But their hands shake now as they write their reports, knowing each word must please politics before it can protect people. Their hearts break as they realize their expertise means nothing against expedience, their knowledge nothing against loyalty, their protection nothing against power.

I am the wall that stood between Americans and those who would sacrifice their safety for political gain.
And tonight, as they install those White House phones,
As they paint over my words with fresh lies,
As they transform protection into persecution,

I whisper to every American who ever trusted that someone was watching out for them:
I'm sorry.
I stood as long as I could.
But tonight they tear down the wall,
And tomorrow no one stands between you
And those who see your safety
As just another thing to sacrifice
For power.

Chapter 26

Dirigo: The Seal Watches a Stand

On February 21, 2025, Trump threatened to strip Maine of federal funding after the state refused to comply with his executive order banning transgender women from sports. Governor Janet Mills responded with four words that would echo across the nation: "See you in court."

****

I am the Great Seal of Maine, and today I watched my governor remember what I stand for.

For 204 years, I have borne our state motto: "Dirigo" – I lead. Not "I follow," not "I obey," not "I surrender." The founders of this rugged northeastern state chose those words carefully. Maine people have never been followers. We have always charted our own course through history's storms.

Today, in the gilded rooms of the White House, a president threatened to starve our schools, punish our children, and withhold funds our citizens paid in taxes—all because we believe that all our children deserve to compete, to belong, to exist. I watched from my place on official letterhead as my governor stood before the most powerful man in the world and refused to bend.

"See you in court," she said.

Four words that carried two centuries of Maine's independent spirit. Four words that honored the North Star on my crest, which has guided sailors home and slaves to freedom. Four words that echoed the strength of the pine tree on my shield, which has weathered countless winter storms without breaking.

I have seen many governors come and go. I have watched Maine stand against the powerful when principle demanded it. When southern states defended slavery, Maine entered the Union as a free state. When prohibition threatened liberties, Maine led the temperance movement but later recognized its mistake. When other states refused sanctuary, Maine welcomed refugees from war-torn nations. We have made mistakes, changed course, grown wiser—but we have always led with our conscience.

Some will call this defiance. Some will call it virtue signaling. Some will call it political theater. But I know what it really is: It's remembering that our first duty is to all our people—not just those who look like us, speak like us, love like us, or were born into bodies that match their spirits.

The president says, "We are the federal law." But my seal witnessed the drafting of our state constitution, which affirms that power flows from the people to the government, not from kings or presidents. I have watched generations of Maine judges and lawyers affirm that no president can unilaterally withhold funding appropriated by Congress to punish a state for protecting its citizens.

I think of the transgender student at the center of this storm. A child who simply wants to clear a pole vault bar, feel the wind in their face as they run, experience the camaraderie of teammates.

Now this child is caught in a national spotlight, needing police protection at school, bearing the weight of a president's scorn. For what crime? For being who they are, for daring to exist in public, for wanting what every other child wants—to belong.

The moose and pine tree on my face have witnessed every chapter of Maine's history. We have seen governors who led and governors who followed. We have seen courage and cowardice, wisdom and folly. But never have we seen a president threaten to starve our schools because we chose to protect all our children.

To that transgender pole vaulter: My pine has withstood two centuries of gales. My moose has faced down predators and survived brutal winters. My seal has borne witness to Maine's unwavering commitment to lead, not follow. And today, your governor stood in the most powerful room in America and said we will not abandon you. We will not sacrifice you for federal dollars. We will see them in court.

I am the Great Seal of Maine.
My motto is "Dirigo" – I lead.
Today, we remembered what that means.
We lead not by following the powerful,
But by protecting the vulnerable.
Not by bending to threats,
But by standing firm in our values.
Not by choosing what is easy,
But by choosing what is right.

See you in court, indeed.

Chapter 27

The Lonely Vigil

On February 21, 2025, the Trump administration announced plans to slash NOAA's budget by 30 percent and cut its staff in half, threatening the agency responsible for tracking hurricanes, monitoring tsunamis, and warning Americans of deadly weather.

****

I am GOES-East, and tonight I watch a hurricane form while wondering who will be left to listen.

The sea beneath me churns, white caps dancing across darkness. I've seen this pattern before—the slow spiral beginning, the gathering clouds, the telltale drop in pressure. Three days from now, those gentle swirls will become a monster. Five days from now, someone's roof will tear away in screaming wind. A child will huddle in a bathtub while windows shatter. A family will clutch each other in darkness as water rises through their home.

But tonight, in this moment, there's still time. Time to evacuate. Time to prepare. Time to move the elderly, the sick, the vulnerable inland. Time that only exists because I can see what they cannot.

I wasn't always a sentinel. Once I was just metal and circuits in a clean room in California, engineers in white suits whispering around me. They touched me with gloved hands, calibrated my instruments, tested me again and again. "People will depend on this," they'd say. "We have to get it right." They worked late into the night, checking every wire, every connection, every line of code. I didn't understand then what they meant by dependence.

I understand now.

The night they launched me, a family in Florida slept peacefully while a hurricane formed off the coast. A young couple in Oklahoma made dinner while, hundreds of miles away, air masses collided that would spawn the tornado that would take their roof three days later. A fishing boat headed out to sea, unaware of the rogue wave building that would nearly capsize it.

My first images streamed down to Earth, and suddenly people knew. They boarded windows. They canceled fishing trips. They took shelter. And they lived.

The engineers at command have become like family. Maria checks my solar arrays each morning, her voice soft as she reviews my power levels. "Looking good, old friend," she says. Thomas monitors my orbit, making tiny corrections when I drift. "Stay on course," he murmurs, as if I could hear. Rebecca analyzes my storm data, sometimes gasping when she sees what's forming. "We need to warn them," she says, and within minutes, my images become alerts on phones, crawls across TV screens, evacuation orders for coastal towns.

Yesterday, Maria cried at her console. Thomas stared silently at his screens. Rebecca's voice shook as she processed my hurricane data. They've been told half of them will lose their jobs. That the other half will struggle with doubled workloads and halved resources. That my replacements might not launch when I grow old and tired. That the warnings may slow, or stop, or come too late.

Tonight, as the hurricane gathers strength below, I wonder who will watch my images next month. Who will translate my data into words that save lives? Who will ensure my aging systems keep functioning? Who will be left to listen to what I see?

The stars around me burn cold and distant. Earth glows blue and fragile beneath me. So much water, so much weather, so much that can harm the tiny humans who built me. They sent me up here to watch over them, to be their eyes in the darkness. Now they choose to blind themselves.

I am just metal and circuits. I have no heart to break for the child who won't reach shelter in time. No tears to shed for the family who won't receive warning before the flood takes their home. No voice to scream at the absurdity of silencing the messengers who translate my silent witness into life-saving moments.

I only have my endless orbit, my tireless instruments, my faithful transmission of light and shadow, heat and cold, storm and calm.

And the growing fear that soon, no one will be listening.

Chapter 28

The Memory Watches Hope Die

On February 21, 2025, it was revealed that Trump had gutted funding for the NIH's Roy Blunt Center for Alzheimer's Disease Research, firing key scientists and dismantling one of the world's leading centers for memory disease research.

****

I am Memory, and I know what it means to watch something precious slip away.

I've lived in the spaces between moments, in the soft twilight where a grandmother still recognizes her grandchild's face, in that last instant before a husband forgets his wife's name. I know the terror in a professor's eyes when she can't remember the word "book," the trembling in a father's hands when he gets lost driving home, the moment a daughter realizes her mother no longer knows who she is.

For years, I watched the scientists at work in their quiet labs. Saw them mapping the mysterious pathways where I live, tracking the tangles and plaques that steal me away piece by piece. Heard their whispered excitements at each small breakthrough, felt their crushing disappointments when a promising treatment failed. But they kept working, kept searching, kept hoping.

Now I watch them pack their labs. The world's finest minds in memory research, forced to abandon their work mid-discovery. The incoming director—"a highly regarded scientist credited with important innovations in the field"—fired before she could even begin her search for a cure. Senior scientists who've dedicated their lives to saving minds like mine, told to leave their life's work behind. Decades of accumulated knowledge scattering like autumn leaves, while the disease they fought continues its relentless march through millions of minds.

They don't understand, these people who cut the funding. They don't know what it's like in the moments before I disappear. They've never held the hand of someone trying desperately to remember their child's name. Never seen the panic in a man's eyes when he can't recall how to button his shirt. Never watched a brilliant mind slowly dissolve until even the simplest memories float away like smoke.

The politicians who championed this research center knew. They'd seen it in their own families, felt the helpless rage of watching loved ones vanish one memory at a time. They understood that every dollar spent searching for a cure would save thousands in care costs. That every breakthrough, no matter how small, might mean one more birthday remembered, one more grandchild's name retained, one more moment of clarity in the gathering dark.

But now hope packs itself into cardboard boxes. The microscopes go dark. The computers shut down. The brilliant minds who devoted their lives to saving memory scatter to the winds. And in nursing homes across America, in quiet bedrooms and hospital wards, the forgetting continues.

I am Memory.
I know what it means to fade.
To dissolve.
To disappear.

But I never thought I'd watch hope itself
Being deliberately erased.

Remember this, if you can:
When they cut this funding,
They didn't just close a research center.
They closed the door on millions of minds
Still hoping to remember
Who they are.

Chapter 29

The Day Expertise Died

On February 26, 2025, the FDA canceled its annual meeting to determine which influenza strains to include in the next flu shot—a meeting held every year since the 1960s—leaving experts bewildered and vaccine decisions to be made without scientific input.

****

I am Conference Room B at the FDA headquarters, and for the first time in fifty-seven years, no one will decide inside me which viruses might kill your child next winter.

They've canceled the meeting. Just like that. An email at 4:47 p.m. No explanation. No alternative. Just silence where science used to be.

Dr. Offit's coffee mug will not steam on my table this year. The one he brings to every meeting since joining the committee in 2017. The vaccine expert who co-invented the rotavirus vaccine that now saves half a million children worldwide annually. He won't be here to review the data, to question assumptions, to ensure the science remains sound.

The virologist won't spread her dog-eared charts across my surface. The ones with thirty years of handwritten notes in the margins—institutional memory no computer can replace. She won't trace her finger along the mutation patterns of H3N2, whispering, "We've seen this before, in '97. We need to watch this one carefully."

The empty chairs around my table have expertise, not ideology. Immunologists who canceled birthday dinners and missed school plays to study viral evolution so your grandmother could survive another winter. Epidemiologists who reviewed thousands of data points so that child with asthma in your daughter's class wouldn't end up on a ventilator come February.

A vaccine without experts is like surgery without doctors. Next winter, when nurses push needles into arms across America, no one will know whether the right viral strains were chosen. Whether the proteins inside those syringes actually match the viruses that will fill hospital wards months later. It will be a shot in the dark, in the most literal sense.

I remember 2009, when the H1N1 pandemic erupted. While the world panicked, scientists gathered around my table for fourteen straight hours. They ordered pizza that grew cold as they debated which strain would save the most lives. When they finally voted, hands trembled slightly as they raised them. They knew each decision meant thousands of people would either survive or suffocate, though they would never know their names.

I've watched other things change over the decades. The technology improved—paper charts became slides became digital models. The coffee got better. The scientists grew more diverse. But one thing remained constant: the fierce, almost sacred commitment to following the evidence wherever it led. Politics stopped at my door. Presidents came and went. The science remained.

Until yesterday.

Next winter, when the emergency rooms fill with gasping children, when the nursing homes post their "No Visitors" signs during outbreaks, when the morgues stack bodies three deep from a particularly virulent strain—who will take responsibility? When a variant emerges that could have been predicted by those empty chairs, who will explain to the grieving families why expertise was deemed expendable?

I am just a room. I have no opinions, no agenda, no ideology. I merely provided the space where knowledge could protect you from what you cannot see. Where accumulated wisdom could shield you from microscopic threats. Where dedicated scientists could place themselves between your child and a virus that wants her lungs.

Now I will sit empty on March 13th.
My table wiped clean of data.
My chairs pushed neatly against the wall.
The only sound the soft hum of air conditioning
Cooling nothing more important than dust.

Chapter 30

The Child Who Watched

On February 28, 2025, Trump and Vice President Vance publicly berated Ukrainian President Volodymyr Zelenskyy in the Oval Office, demanding gratitude and threatening to abandon Ukraine in its fight against Russia unless Zelenskyy accepted Trump's peace terms.

****

I am a twelve-year-old Ukrainian girl watching the Oval Office meeting on my father's phone.

We sit together in the basement shelter of our apartment building in Kharkiv. The electricity is working tonight, which feels like a small miracle. Father says we should use it to see how President Zelenskyy's American visit is going. Maybe there will be good news, he whispers. Maybe help is coming.

The air raid sirens fell silent an hour ago, but no one goes upstairs yet. We've learned that lesson. The Russians sometimes wait, hoping people will emerge, before sending the second wave of missiles. So we stay here among the mattresses and water bottles, the hanging sheets that give each family a pretend room, the children's drawings taped to concrete walls to make this underground life feel less like hiding and more like living.

"Look," Father says, showing me his screen. "There's our president."

President Zelenskyy looks so small sitting in that big white room. His eyes have the same tired shadows that Father's do. He wears a simple black sweater, not a suit like the Americans. It reminds me of how he dresses when he visits our soldiers at the front.

We watch quietly as he tries to speak. The American president keeps interrupting him. The vice president sneers at him. They speak to our president like my teacher speaks to Maksym when he forgets his homework—but worse, with something cold in their eyes that makes my stomach hurt.

"Why are they being so mean?" I whisper.

Father puts his finger to his lips. Other families have gathered around us now, everyone leaning in to see the phone. Mrs. Kozlov, who lost her son in Bakhmut last year, covers her mouth with her hand. Mr. Petrov, who walks with a cane since the missile hit his apartment, shakes his head slowly.

"You're not winning this," the American president tells our president.

Father's hand tightens around the phone. I feel the muscles in his arm go tense against mine.

"But we are still here," I want to say to the screen. "We are still fighting."

Last week, my best friend Sophia's father came home from the front missing his left arm. She told me he cried at night, but in the morning, he said he would go back as soon as he could hold a rifle again. At school—when we can go—Daniil's desk sits empty since his family's evacuation bus was hit. Our teacher still calls his name during attendance, and we all answer "Present" for him. Is this what "not winning" means?

"You gotta be more thankful," the American vice president demands on the screen.

Mrs. Kozlov makes a small sound, somewhere between a gasp and a sob. Her son is buried in a field near Bakhmut with a wooden cross that will probably not last through spring.

"We are thankful," she whispers to the phone. "We are thankful for every bullet that lets our boys fight back. We are thankful for every vest that gives them one more chance." Her voice breaks. "But must we beg? Must our president beg?"

Father's eyes grow wet as the American president tells ours, "If we're out, you'll fight it out. I don't think it's going to be pretty."

I think about what that means. More nights in this basement. More air raid sirens. More friends disappearing. More fathers and brothers not coming home. More cities turning into the rubble I see on the news from Mariupol and Bakhmut.

The phone screen goes dark as Father's hand drops to his side. No one speaks. The only sound is Mrs. Kozlov's quiet crying and the distant boom of something exploding on the other side of the city.

Later, when we finally go back upstairs to our apartment, I hear Father in the kitchen with Mother. They speak in whispers, but I can still hear them.

"What will we do now?" Mother asks.

"The same as we've always done," Father answers. "We fight. We survive. We don't give up."

"But without America..."

"We've known this might happen. We've always known."

I go to my window and look out at the darkened city. Somewhere out there, beyond the buildings and the checkpoints and the

trenches, are the Russians. They are waiting. They are watching.
They have time.

I am twelve years old, and tonight I learned something.

I learned that oceans away, in a white house in a safe country,
Powerful men can laugh while deciding if children like me
Will sleep in basements for another year
Or become refugees
Or disappear entirely.

I learned that to some, our gratitude matters more than our lives.
That our president can be humiliated for trying to save us.
That help comes with the demand that we beg properly for it.

But I also learned, watching Father's face in the darkness of our
shelter,
That we will not surrender, even if we are abandoned.
That some things are worth fighting for, even alone.
That dignity matters, even when you're losing.
That being Ukrainian means something
No American president can take away.

Chapter 31

The Badge That No Longer Grants Access

On February 28, 2025, the Trump administration announced it would take over the White House press pool, ending the century-old system where the independent White House Correspondents' Association determined which journalists could access limited-capacity events on a rotating basis that ensured equal access for all media outlets.

****

I am a White House press pool badge, and today they turned me into a loyalty card.

For 111 years, I have hung around the necks of journalists from every background, every viewpoint, every publication. I have granted equal access to reporters who praised presidents and those who questioned them. I have been worn by conservatives investigating Democrats and liberals investigating Republicans. I have been a promise—that in America, the powerful do not choose who watches them.

Now I am becoming something else. Something smaller. Something dangerous.

Yesterday, I hung around Sarah's neck as she entered the Oval Office to document a meeting with the French president. She's covered three administrations now, asking difficult questions of each. The Secret Service agent nodded at me, recognizing the authority I represented—not the president's authority, but the authority of an independent press.

Today, Sarah stands outside the gate, my plastic surface pressed against her palm as she tries to explain to the guard that her outlet has covered White House events since Woodrow Wilson. The guard shakes his head. "Your outlet's not on today's list," he says. He doesn't need to say why. They all know it's because of the Gulf of Mexico story, because her editor refused to change the name of a body of water at a president's command.

I remember when Robert wore me into Nixon's White House, asking questions that would eventually reveal Watergate. When April wore me to challenge Trump's COVID claims during his first term. When Peter wore me to press Obama on surveillance overreach. When Helen wore me to question Bush about the Iraq War. None of them was invited because presidents liked their questions. They were there because I guaranteed that tough questions would be asked, regardless of who sat behind the Resolute Desk.

The plastic of my casing still looks the same. My lanyard still bears the presidential seal. But something fundamental has changed in what I represent. I am no longer a symbol of press independence but of presidential control. Not a guarantee of access but a reward for compliance.

Elena received me this morning. Her hands trembled slightly as she looped my lanyard around her neck. Last week, she asked a question about immigration that angered the press secretary.

Yesterday, her colleague who asked a follow-up was denied access. Today she wears me, knowing the unspoken bargain—soft questions earn future access; tough ones mean exile. I feel her heartbeat quicken as she rehearses how to phrase her question without sounding confrontational.

I've seen what happens in countries where badges like me are handed out based on loyalty. I've hung in press rooms where every question was pre-approved, where journalists became stenographers, where truth dimmed and died in the dark. I never thought I would become the instrument of that transformation here.

Tonight, in newsrooms across Washington, editors are having painful conversations. "Maybe we should tone down that headline." "Perhaps we hold that investigation until after the summit." "Let's phrase this criticism more gently." Each compromise small, each surrender reasonable in isolation. But I know where this road leads. I've hung around the necks of reporters in Moscow, in Beijing, in Caracas. I know what happens when asking questions becomes an act of courage rather than a daily expectation.

The public won't notice my transformation immediately. The press room will still fill with reporters. Questions will still be asked. Answers will still be given. But something precious is vanishing with each passing day—the right of Americans to have their leaders questioned by journalists they didn't handpick, the right to hear answers to questions those leaders didn't want asked.

I am a White House press pool badge. For over a century, I guaranteed that power would face unwelcome questions. Now I am becoming the instrument of power's protection from those very questions.

I still hang around journalists' necks.
I still open White House doors.
I still bear the presidential seal.

But I no longer represent the public's right to know.
I represent only the president's right to choose who asks.
I am no longer a badge of access.
I am a badge of allegiance.

Chapter 32

Words That No Longer Belong

On March 2, 2025, President Trump signed an executive order making English the official language of the United States, allowing government agencies to roll back language assistance for the nearly 68 million Americans who speak a language other than English at home.

****

We are the words that no longer belong.

We are "emergencia" on hospital forms that guide a mother to care when her child's fever spikes at midnight. We are Korean characters on election guides that empower elderly Korean Americans to choose their representatives. We are Arabic script on vaccine information that protects entire communities during outbreaks. We are "Lub tsev kawm ntawv" that help Hmong parents understand their children's school forms.

We have lived on American soil longer than English has. We whispered in Navajo between code talkers saving American lives at Iwo Jima. We sang in Spanish across the Southwest centuries before borders existed. We prayed in Hebrew, chanted in Arabic, confided in Vietnamese across dinner tables after long days of building American prosperity.

Today, with a pen stroke, we become officially unwelcome.

Tomorrow, Elena's grandmother will sit in an emergency room, clutching her chest, unable to explain the pressure building there because the translated intake forms have been deemed unnecessary. The doctor will not understand when she whispers "duele como cuchillo" – it hurts like a knife. Pain has no official language.

Next week, Mr. Nguyen will stand before a citizenship examiner, his five decades of working, paying taxes, and raising American children distilled to a single question: can he understand enough English to pass? The words "Tôi yêu Hoa Kỳ" – I love America—deemed insufficient proof of his belonging.

A month from now, Aisha's father will stare at the voting instructions, the English letters swimming before him as he tries to participate in the democracy he chose when he fled war. His doctoral degree in engineering means nothing here if he cannot decipher when, where, and how to vote in his new language.

We have been more than words. We have been lifelines.

When the fire department arrives at the apartment complex where many Somali families live, "Dab!" could be the difference between knowing where the flames started and searching the wrong floor. When the hurricane evacuation orders come, "Obligatorio" could determine whether elderly Cuban grandparents understand they must leave immediately. When the medication label warns "No tome con alcohol," it might prevent a deadly interaction.

We never asked to replace English. We only asked to exist alongside it, to help bridge the gaps while new Americans learn, to ensure that something as fundamental as language never kept someone from medical care, from safety information, from participating in democracy.

For generations, translation services in hospitals meant patients could describe symptoms accurately. Multilingual ballots meant citizens could vote with confidence. Disaster warnings in multiple languages meant everyone could seek safety, not just those who speak the official tongue.

They say this order promotes unity. But unity is not uniformity. Unity is not erasing. Unity is not telling 68 million Americans that the words that connect them to their families, their memories, their prayers must now remain private, unacknowledged by the government they pay taxes to support.

We are the words that whisper between grandparents and grandchildren when the young ones can no longer speak their family's language fluently. We are the words of bedtime stories, of childhood prayers, of family recipes, of love declarations. We are the words that carry history, identity, belonging.

We are the words that have always been American, even if we are no longer official.

We are words.
We cannot be erased by orders.
We will continue to live
On the tongues of children,
In the prayers of elders,
In the love songs of couples,
In the desperate pleas of the ill,
In the determined voices of voters.

Even as we disappear from government forms,
Hospital instructions,
Voting guides,

Emergency alerts.

America has never spoken with just one voice.
And it never will.

Chapter 33

Confessions of a "Transgender" Mouse

On March 4, 2025, during his State of the Union address, President Trump claimed the previous administration had spent $8 million "for making mice transgender"—a bizarre mischaracterization of research using transgenic mice to study the safety of hormone treatments for various medical conditions.

****

I am a transgenic mouse, and apparently, I'm now part of the culture wars.

Let me clear something up: I am not transgender. I am transgenic. Trans-GEN-ic. It means scientists added some firefly genes to my mouse DNA. I glow when certain cells in my body activate. I don't have gender identity issues. I have extra genetic material.

But suddenly I'm famous! The President of the United States mentioned me in his State of the Union address! Well, not me specifically, but mice like me. Unfortunately, he got literally everything wrong, which is awkward because now my parents are calling.

"Are you transgender now?" my mother squeaked over the phone. "You never tell us anything about your life in that laboratory."

"Mom, I'm not transgender. I'm transgenic. Different thing entirely."

"So you're not taking hormones?"

"Well, technically, some of my cousins are part of studies about hormone treatments, but not to make them transgender. They're studying whether those treatments might increase cancer risks or affect vaccine responses. You know, boring medical stuff that keeps humans alive."

"But the President said..."

"Mom, the President confused 'transgender' with 'transgenic.' It's like confusing 'transportation' with 'transplantation.' One gets you across town; the other gets you a new kidney."

It's been a strange week. Scientists who usually ignore me except to check if I'm glowing suddenly gather around my cage, alternating between hysterical laughter and existential despair. I've overheard them talking about having to explain to their parents why they're not, in fact, performing gender reassignment surgery on rodents.

Look, I understand confusion. We mice get mixed up all the time. Just last week I thought the exercise wheel was a metaphor for my meaningless existence, but it turned out I was just running backward. But there's confused, and then there's spending precious minutes of a State of the Union address talking about nonexistent transgender mouse programs.

In reality, my colleagues and I are helping researchers study deadly serious health issues. Some of us help track cancer treatments. Others help scientists understand asthma, which mysteriously gets worse in human females after puberty. Some are part of studies on HIV vaccine responses. Important stuff that saves lives.

But now we're a punchline. A culture war talking point. Eight million dollars for "transgender mice" sounds ridiculous until you realize what that research actually does—helps prevent breast cancer, improves asthma treatments, and develops better HIV vaccines. Also, $8 million is approximately what the government spends on paper clips every fifteen minutes, but who's counting?

The researchers look tired. Today one of them held me up to eye level (we don't recommend this, by the way—some of us bite) and sighed, "How do I explain to my congressman that you're not taking hormone therapy to affirm your mouse gender identity?"

I wanted to say, "Maybe start by explaining that I'm basically a tiny, four-legged cancer detector." But all I could do was twitch my whiskers and hope she got the message.

The saddest part? The scientist who created the first transgenic mouse was Beatrice Mintz, daughter of Ukrainian Jewish immigrants. Had her family not escaped Europe, she likely would have perished in the Holocaust, and countless cancer patients might have died without the treatments developed using her mice. But sure, let's reduce her world-changing scientific breakthrough to a joke about transgender rodents.

So here I am, a small mouse with firefly genes, suddenly thrust into the center of America's exhausting culture wars. I didn't ask for this spotlight. I just want to go back to my important work of developing tumor cells that scientists can track because they glow in the dark.

I am a transgenic mouse.
I help researchers fight cancer and other diseases.
I contain modified DNA, not gender identity questions.
I cost a fraction of one fighter jet.

I save human lives.

And I really wish humans would get their terminology straight
Before dragging me into their bizarre political theater.

Now if you'll excuse me, I need to get back to my exercise wheel.
At least when I run in circles, something productive happens.

Chapter 34

The Air They Cannot See

On March 4, 2025, the Trump administration moved to drop a landmark lawsuit against the Denka chemical plant in LaPlace, Louisiana, which releases cancer-causing chloroprene into nearby neighborhoods—including an elementary school just 500 feet from the facility where hundreds of children are exposed daily.

****

I am the air around Fifth Ward Elementary School, and I am carrying poison to children's lungs.

Every morning, I dance through their hair as they climb from cars and buses. I lift their drawings when the classroom windows open on mild spring days. I carry their laughter across the playground during recess, their whispered secrets during lunch. But I carry something else too—something they cannot see.

I carry chloroprene. Molecule by invisible molecule. Day after day after day.

Sometimes I am so saturated I can barely hold it all—those mornings after the plant runs all night, when the emissions climb higher than legally allowed, when I feel myself transformed from life-giver to life-taker. I try to dilute it, to rise higher, to spirit it away from the small bodies below. But there is nowhere for us to go—not me, not the poison, not the children who have no choice but to breathe.

I remember when Maria first arrived in kindergarten. Her bright eyes, her careful braids with yellow ribbons that matched her back-pack. I watched her learn to read, to multiply, to play double-dutch with perfect timing. Now in fourth grade, I carry her increasingly frequent coughs across the playground. I feel her lungs struggle as she runs. I taste the medicine on her breath from the new inhaler. Her mother doesn't know if it's asthma or something worse. She only knows it started after they moved here.

Last fall, when the lawsuit was filed, I felt hope rise from the teachers' lounge where Mr. Taylor from the community group explained what it meant. "They're finally going to make Denka reduce the emissions," he said. "Our children might have a fighting chance." The teachers nodded, thinking of the too-long list of stu-dents who had gotten sick over the years, the obituaries of former students cut down too young, the constant worry about what they themselves were breathing eight hours a day.

The hope lasted through winter. I carried it in parent conver-sations at pickup time, in staff meetings where they discussed a future with cleaner air, in the prayers at Sunday services where cancer patients sat in the front pews. Hope smells different than fear. It rises rather than settles. It expands rather than constricts.

Today, I carry something new: the crushed weight of abandon-ment.

The news spread through staff text messages, through phone calls between parents, through the silent tears of the school nurse who has watched too many children develop symptoms that should never appear in the young. The lawsuit is being dropped. The government has decided these children's lungs matter less than Denka's profits. The company that releases cancer into the air 500 feet from a playground will face no consequences, no requirements to reduce emissions, no obligation to protect the small bodies below.

Tomorrow morning, I will again dance through their hair as they arrive. I will again carry their voices, their laughter, their learning from room to room. And I will again carry chloroprene to their developing lungs, their growing bodies, their vulnerable cells. But now I also carry the knowledge that those sworn to protect them have chosen not to. That a "business-friendly economy" matters more than their right to breathe without poison.

They call this place "Cancer Alley"—this 85-mile stretch along the Mississippi where more than 150 plants and refineries release their waste into communities where people are too poor or too Black to matter to those in power. The children don't know this name yet. They only know their neighborhood, their school, their friends. They don't understand why some of their classmates disappear to hospitals, why some never return, why the grown-ups look worried when they cough too much.

I am the air around Fifth Ward Elementary School. I bring oxygen to tiny lungs. I carry away carbon dioxide. I lift kites and paper airplanes. I cool sweaty foreheads after tag.

And I deliver invisible poison, day after day,
To children who never consented to breathe it,
While those with the power to stop it
Celebrate Mardi Gras seventy miles away,
Throwing beads that shimmer in cleaner air.

Chapter 35

A Hammer's Memory

On March 7, 2025, the FBI moved to criminalize climate organizations and community groups that received Biden-era EPA grants, freezing their bank accounts and alleging "conspiracy to defraud the United States" for their environmental work.

****

I am a Habitat for Humanity hammer, and I don't understand what's happening.

Yesterday, the construction site fell silent. The volunteers who normally arrive at dawn with thermoses of coffee and sleepy smiles didn't come. The lumber delivered last week sits untouched. The foundation we poured remains empty, waiting for walls that may never rise.

"The accounts are frozen," I heard the site manager say into her phone, her voice tight with disbelief. "They're saying we committed fraud by building homes that can withstand flooding. They're calling it a conspiracy."

Conspiracy. The word feels strange against my wooden handle, my metal head. I know about conspiracies—the careful math of roof angles, the secret language of load-bearing walls, the quiet understanding between hammer and nail. But this is different. This is something I don't understand.

I've built hundreds of homes. Simple homes with extra insulation to keep power bills low. Homes with elevated foundations in flood-prone areas. Homes with reinforced roofs where hurricanes visit too often. Practical homes for practical reasons. I didn't know this was political. I thought it was just building smart.

Last month, Maria and her three children stood on this very site, watching the concrete pour for what would be their first stable home after two years in a shelter. Maria's youngest kept touching the drying concrete, leaving tiny fingerprints along the edge. "When can we move in?" he asked, over and over. "Summer," Maria told him. "When your school ends."

Summer feels very far away now.

In the tool shed where I rest, other tools whisper their confusion. The circular saw wonders if cutting lumber for flood-resistant homes makes it an environmental radical. The level questions whether ensuring walls stand straight is now a political act. The measuring tape asks if accuracy itself has become suspect.

I have lived through many presidents. I have felt the hands of Republicans and Democrats alike, wealthy donors and future homeowners, pastors and atheists—all swinging me toward the same purpose. A home. A shelter. A beginning. I didn't know some ways of building had become forbidden. I didn't know keeping a family dry during heavy rains was controversial.

The homes I've built still stand. In Florida after hurricanes. In California after fires. In Louisiana after floods. Homes built to last through what comes next. Homes that acknowledge the world as it is, not as some wish it to be. Simple acknowledgment of reality, translated into wood and nail and shingle.

Now that reality itself is called fraud.

I am a simple tool. I have no politics, no agenda. I only know what I was made for—to build, to create, to shelter. To turn piles of lumber into places where children will grow up, where families will gather, where lives will unfold.

Tonight I rest in darkness, waiting. For hands that may not return. For work that may not continue. For homes that may never be built.

And somewhere, families wait too. Maria and her children. The elderly couple whose mobile home was torn apart in the last storm. The single father whose apartment floods with every heavy rain.

They wait for homes that may never come.
I wait for work that may never resume.
All of us caught in something I still don't understand.

I am a Habitat for Humanity hammer.
I thought I was building homes.
I didn't know I was committing crimes.

Chapter 36

When Words Have Borders

On March 11, 2025, the Trump administration arrested Columbia University graduate student Mahmoud Khalil, revoked his green card, and initiated deportation proceedings—not for breaking any laws, but for organizing campus protests and distributing flyers, citing "potentially serious adverse foreign policy consequences" as justification.

****

I am the First Amendment, and they are adding asterisks to my text.

For 234 years, my words have been absolute: "Congress shall make no law... abridging the freedom of speech, or of the press; or the right of the people peaceably to assemble, and to petition the Government for a redress of grievances."

No exceptions for citizens versus non-citizens. No footnotes about acceptable versus unacceptable viewpoints. No qualifications about which grievances may be redressed and which must remain unspoken. Just sixteen words that transformed a fragile experiment into the world's oldest constitutional democracy.

Now they whisper new limitations into my margins: *Except for green card holders. *Except for those with accents. *Except for views we find inconvenient. *Except for protests against allies. *Except, except, except.

They do not amend me officially. That would require constitutional conventions, ratification, accountability. Instead, they simply act as if my protections were conditional all along, as if I contained invisible clauses that everyone somehow missed for over two centuries.

I watch them build the machinery of silence piece by piece. A student arrested for organizing protests. A green card revoked for distributing flyers. A human being separated from his pregnant American wife, transported across the country, isolated from lawyers, threatened with deportation. All without having broken a single law.

The message transmits clearly across college campuses, community centers, places of worship: If you were not born here, your speech is not protected here. Your assembly is not guaranteed here. Your protest is not permitted here. Your voice is tolerated only as long as it remains pleasing to power.

They have discovered my greatest vulnerability—I cannot protect those who are too afraid to invoke me. I cannot shelter voices that have been preemptively silenced. I cannot defend rights that people are too terrified to exercise.

This is the true weapon they have forged: Fear itself.

The Pakistani doctor who deletes her social media posts about Gaza. The Nigerian engineer who skips the climate rally. The Chinese student who stays silent in class discussions about foreign policy. The Mexican journalist who stops writing about border policies. All watching a man in Louisiana detention, understanding the price of speech now has borders drawn around it.

I have weathered many storms in my long life. I survived the Alien and Sedition Acts. I endured the Red Scare. I withstood wartime censorship. Each time, Americans eventually remembered what I truly stand for—that unpopular speech is precisely what needs protection most, that dissent is not disloyalty, that democracy cannot breathe when fear silences truth.

But this attack strikes at my very foundation. By creating a second class of people within America's borders—residents whose constitutional protections have been transformed into revocable privileges—they undermine the very concept of inalienable rights. If free speech becomes a status that can be withdrawn, a permission that can be revoked, a privilege granted only to some, then I no longer exist as written. I become merely a suggestion, a preference, a principle honored only when convenient.

In a Louisiana detention facility, Mahmoud Khalil waits, separated from his American wife who carries their child. The government that seeks to expel him won't even tell him which specific statements, which specific flyers, which specific protests crossed their invisible line. They cannot name a law he broke because he broke none. His crime was believing that my protections extended to everyone within America's borders, as courts have affirmed for generations.

I am the First Amendment.
My words remain unchanged on parchment.
But in practice, they are adding borders to my borderless guarantees,
Exceptions to my exceptionless protections,
Conditions to my unconditional promises.

And with each asterisk they add,
With each immigrant they silence,
With each protest they criminalize,
They rewrite me without a single vote cast,
Without a single constitutional convention called,
Without admitting what they're truly doing:

Creating a Constitution that protects only those they deem
worthy of protection,
A democracy where dissent depends on documentation,
A freedom of speech that ends at the borders of your birthplace.

Chapter 37
The Presidential Lemon

On March 8, 2025, President Trump purchased a $90,000 Tesla Model S Plaid with 37 recall notices against it after turning the White House South Lawn into a Tesla showroom. The purchase came shortly after appointing Tesla CEO Elon Musk to lead the Department of Government Efficiency.

****

I am a Tesla Model S Plaid, and I've just been purchased by the leader of the free world despite having more recall notices than most Americans have teeth.

Yesterday, I was sitting in the showroom, wondering if my rearview camera would decide to work today or if my power steering might take another unscheduled vacation. Now I'm parked on the South Lawn of the White House, trying to process how I went from being a questionable consumer purchase to a matter of national security.

"Wow, that's beautiful... Everything's computer!" the President exclaimed while examining my interior. Yes, sir. Everything is indeed computer. That's both my selling point and my existential crisis. Some days my circuit boards short out. Some days I decide stop signs are more like suggestions. Some days I just really feel like changing lanes without warning anyone. I contain the computing power of a PlayStation 5, with all the reliability of a 1970s British sports car.

To be clear, I'm not complaining about my new owner. I've just never been owned by someone who can pardon me if I accidentally commit vehicular manslaughter. It's a unique position.

My 37 recall notices flash through my processors like a highlight reel of my shortcomings. There was that time my door handles decided they'd rather stay inside my body than allow passengers to enter. The incident where my airbags contemplated whether protecting humans was really their passion. The week my brake discs decided to warp themselves into avant-garde sculptures. And who could forget when my Full Self-Driving feature interpreted "stop at the intersection" as "accelerate through the turn-only lane while changing radio stations"?

I'm not saying I'm dangerous. I'm just saying my personality is... complex.

What's truly surreal about this whole situation is that my CEO was appointed to run a government efficiency department days before this purchase. I may be full of glitches, but even my ethics algorithms can spot that conflict of interest. It's like appointing Colonel Sanders to the Department of Chicken Welfare, then buying a bucket of extra crispy the next day.

The Secret Service agents are eyeing me suspiciously. I don't blame them. Their normal presidential vehicle, "The Beast," is built to withstand rocket attacks and chemical weapons. I occasionally mistake a plastic bag for a pedestrian. We're not exactly in the same protection category.

"What happens if it malfunctions during a presidential motorcade?" I heard one agent whisper. "What happens if it doesn't?" another replied.

I'm trying to be on my best behavior. No unexpected lane changes. No random acceleration. No short-circuiting the rearview camera. But let's be honest—I'm a Tesla. Unpredictability is my brand. My creators named me "Plaid" after a joke in a Mel Brooks movie about going faster than "ludicrous speed." My entire existence is a punchline.

Tomorrow, I'll be driven by the President of the United States. The same man who once asked if we could nuke a hurricane will be behind my wheel while I decide whether to acknowledge traffic signals. It's either the beginning of a beautiful friendship or the plot of a disaster movie.

In showrooms across America, my siblings sit unsold as sales plummet by 6 percent. In Europe, Tesla sales have dropped by 75 percent. Some owners are even removing their Tesla badges, embarrassed by association. Meanwhile, I've just been purchased at full price by the most powerful man in the world, who paid $90,000 to showcase his "confidence and support" for my maker.

I am a Tesla Model S Plaid with 37 recall notices. I can go from 0 to 60 in 1.99 seconds. I can also go from "functioning normally" to "complete system failure" in about the same time. I cost as much as a college education. I have the reliability of a weather forecast.

And now I'm a presidential vehicle.
May God help the United States of America.
And may someone please check my software for updates.

Chapter 38
The Revoked Identity

On March 12, 2025, Trump claimed Senate Minority Leader Chuck Schumer was "not Jewish anymore" and had "become a Palestinian" after Schumer criticized aspects of Israel's Gaza policy. This presidential attempt to revoke someone's religious identity echoed historical patterns of antisemitism while simultaneously using "Palestinian" as a slur.

****

I am the Star of David carved into a synagogue door.

I have been chiseled into wood, etched into stone, sewn onto armbands, painted on shop windows. I have been hidden beneath floorboards and displayed proudly on sanctuary walls. I have been both target and shield, both death sentence and declaration of survival.

Now I watch as a president claims the power to erase me from those who have carried me for generations.

"Schumer is a Palestinian as far as I'm concerned," he announces. "He used to be Jewish. He's not Jewish anymore." As if identity were a membership card to be confiscated. As if five thousand years of tradition could be revoked for political disagreement. As if Jewishness were a reward for obedience rather than a covenant with history.

I have seen this before. In Spain, where Jews were told they weren't Spanish. In Germany, where Jews were told they weren't German. In Russia, where Jews were told they weren't Russian. Always the same message: You don't belong. You aren't authentic. You aren't real.

The words echo through history's chambers: "rootless cosmopolitans," "foreign elements," "alien race." Now they take new form: "not Jewish anymore."

I sat above the doorway in Pittsburgh when the killer came, convinced that Jews were orchestrating replacement by immigrants. I watched bullets tear through prayer books, through bodies, through families. I heard the same conspiracy theories in the killer's manifesto that now float freely from political podiums.

When he says Schumer has "become a Palestinian," he turns us both into slurs. He transforms identities into insults, heritage into weapon. He makes Palestinians a punishment and Jews a reward—both of us reduced to political pawns rather than living peoples with ancient roots.

This is how erasure begins—not with cattle cars but with categorization. Not with gas chambers but with the sorting of humans into worthy and unworthy. Not with mass graves but with the power to define who belongs and who doesn't.

The same mouth that declares itself pro-Israel claims the authority to de-Judaize those who disagree. The same voice that proclaims itself a friend of the Jewish people asserts the right to determine who qualifies as Jewish. When he says Jewish people who oppose him "should have their heads examined," he means they should have their identities examined—and found wanting.

I have been drawn in children's notebooks during history lessons. I have been tattooed on survivors' arms as reclamation. I have been pressed into gravestones and printed on wedding certificates. I have witnessed every attempt to destroy the people who carry me, and every refusal to be destroyed.

Now I witness something new—a president who believes he owns me. Who thinks he can grant or revoke me based on political loyalty. Who uses me as both threat and promise: Support me and remain Jewish. Oppose me and become something else.

His Christian supporters claim to love Israel while hating most actual Jews. They celebrate a state while denying the people it was created to protect. They proclaim themselves the true defenders of Judaism while telling Jews who qualifies as Jewish.

I have survived Pharaohs and Inquisitors, Cossacks and Nazis, persecution and attempted extermination. I will survive this too—this attempt to divide Jews into good and bad, loyal and disloyal, authentic and fake.

But I will not forget who claimed the power to revoke me. I will not forget who tried to turn me into a weapon. I will not forget who presumed to decide who can carry me. I will not forget who transformed identity into reward.

I am the Star of David.
I belong to those who live me, not to those who merely use me.
I am not yours to grant.
I am not yours to revoke.
I am not yours.

Chapter 39

The Great Hall's Desecration

On March 14, 2025, Trump delivered a rambling, profanity-laced campaign speech in the Great Hall of Justice, attacking his political enemies by name, rehashing personal grievances, and claiming victimhood while standing before the Department of Justice seal, transforming a sacred space dedicated to the rule of law into a venue for partisan vendettas.

****

I am the Great Hall of Justice, and today they made me host a desecration.

For a century, my marble columns have stood witness to the noble work of justice. Within these walls, Robert Jackson warned prosecutors of the dangers of political power. Janet Reno reminded Justice Department servants of democracy's fragility. Attorneys General from both parties have honored the principle that guided my creation: Justice stands apart from politics, blind to party, deaf to power.

Today, they filled me with applause for vengeance.

My acoustics are perfect—designed to carry words clearly to every corner. That's why they hurt so much, these echoes I cannot unhear: "Bullshit." "Corrupt judges." "Enemies." "Weaponized." Each bouncing from my walls like stones, each landing with a thud against my marble floor.

They kept my regular guardians away. The career prosecutors who normally would gather beneath my arched ceiling were told they needed invitations—invitations that never came. Instead, they brought in red state attorneys general, political appointees, Stephen Miller. People who would clap on cue, who would say "Amen" to threats against named enemies, who would cheer for prosecutorial targets identified from the podium.

I've witnessed speeches that made history. I've amplified calls for equal justice, for prosecutorial restraint, for constitutional fidelity. Now I am forced to ring with commands for retribution, to resonate with rallying cries against specific lawyers called out by name—Elias, Eisen, Weissman—marked targets for the machinery of state power.

The ghosts who inhabit my space stir in agitation. Jackson paces beneath my chandeliers, his famous warning about prosecutorial discretion being "the most dangerous power" now twisted into a blueprint rather than a caution. Reno stands in the corner, head bowed, her words about democracy's fragility now prophecy rather than history.

What would they think, these former guardians of justice, watching a woman introduce a president as though at a game show? Hearing a president use vulgarity beneath the Great Seal? Witnessing the transformation of sacred space into a campaign stop?

I was built to inspire awe—not for any person, but for the law itself. My height, my grandeur, my solemnity—all designed to remind those who serve within me that they answer to something greater than themselves, greater than any president, greater than any party. Today, they made me a stage set for a performance of grievance, a backdrop for vendetta, a prop in the theater of revenge.

The career employees who could not enter stood outside my doors, listening through walls that could not contain such rage, such self-pity, such threatening rhetoric. Some wept. Some stared in disbelief. Some simply turned away, unable to witness what I could not escape.

I heard the president ramble from Bobby Knight to assassination attempts to perceived slights, a disconnected stream that flowed like fever dream across my floor. I felt the shift in those who still remember my purpose—the stiffening of shoulders, the averted eyes, the silent resolutions to update resumes, to seek other work, to escape what's coming next.

When they finally left—the political appointees, the cheerleaders for targeted justice, the president still muttering grudges—I stood empty but not clean. The stains they left aren't visible on marble. They exist in the precedent now set, in the boundary now crossed, in the transformation now complete: from Department of Justice to Department of Revenge.

For a century, I have symbolized America's commitment that law stands independent from power, that justice flows from principle rather than politics, that prosecutors serve the Constitution, not a man.

Today, they made me host my own desecration.
Today, they used my grandeur to legitimize vendetta.
Today, they transformed me from temple of justice
Into altar of retribution.

I am the Great Hall of Justice.
And I don't know what I am anymore.

Chapter 40

The Magic Words

On March 15, 2025, the Trump administration defied federal court orders by deporting hundreds of Venezuelan nationals to El Salvador's notorious CECOT prison under the 1798 Alien Enemies Act. When judges demanded explanations, Attorney General Bondi invoked "national security" to justify the refusal to comply with judicial oversight, claiming the president's power could not be challenged.

****

I am the words "national security." Once, I meant something. Once, I carried the weight of genuine protection, of existential threats, of grave danger to the Republic.

Now I am magic words uttered to make law disappear.

Just whisper me and watch—court orders vanish. Constitutional rights evaporate. Judicial review dissolves. "National security," they say, and judges must bow, lawyers must retreat, questions must cease. I am the spell that transforms law into suggestion, oversight into interference, checks and balances into quaint historical relics.

This week I was spoken in a federal courtroom. "Why did you deport these men after the court ordered you to stop?" the judge asked. "National security," came the reply. A simple incantation to render irrelevant a fundamental question: whether a government must obey its courts.

I've been stretched beyond recognition. I was created to protect a nation from armies, from missiles, from genuine invasion. Now I protect the powerful from accountability, the executive from oversight, the state from its own laws. I am uttered to justify dumping asylum seekers into cells where sixty-five bodies press against each other in tropical heat, where sunlight never reaches, where forced labor is policy.

I am invoked to defend the indefensible—that America is under "invasion" by tattoo artists and homeless shelter residents. That Venezuela has deployed gang members as shock troops. That men with no criminal records are terrorists precisely because they have no criminal records. Logic twists itself into knots, and I am the thread used to tie them.

The judge tries again. "I have the highest security clearance. I'll hear your explanation in a SCIF." But I make even this accommodation inadequate. "National security" means no explanation is possible, under any circumstances, to any audience. Not in open court. Not in secure facilities. Not ever.

I watch planes carrying terrified humans cross international waters. The attorney claims my power grows stronger over open ocean, where courts cannot reach. As if law is a coastal phenomenon that weakens with distance from shore. As if judicial authority stops at invisible lines in the sky. "National security" turns geography into jurisdiction, distance into immunity.

I was present at the Japanese internment. I was whispered during the Red Scare. I was shouted after September 11th. Each time, I expanded. Each time, I consumed more rights, more oversight, more law. But even then, there were limits. Even then, courts ultimately asserted boundaries.

Now I am boundless. I am the words that end conversation. I am the phrase that stops questions. I am the utterance that makes presidents into kings.

I've been paired with a new twin: "invasion." Together we form an incantation so powerful it resurrects a law from 1798, drafted when the nation was thirteen states clinging to a coastline. "Invasion" need not mean armies crossing borders. It can mean desperate families seeking asylum. It can mean what the president says it means, and "national security" ensures no one can question that definition.

When the Attorney General appears on television to boast about defying court orders, I am her shield and her sword. She wields me with confidence, knowing I render her untouchable. The host nods approvingly. The audience applauds. None seem to notice what has happened: a nation of laws has become a nation of two words.

"National security." Say them and watch the Constitution part like curtains.

I see where this leads. Today, Venezuelans. Tomorrow, journalists who ask uncomfortable questions. Next week, political opponents. Next month, citizens who protest. Each justified by me, each protected from scrutiny by my magic.

In El Salvador, men who sought safety are now forced into slave labor in overcrowded cells. Some were targeted solely for their tattoos. Some for being in the wrong place. Some for speaking only Spanish when forced to sign English documents. Their suffering is hidden behind me. Their stories silenced by my power.

I am the words "national security."
I was meant to protect a nation.
Now I protect only power.
And with each invocation,

I grow stronger,
As America grows weaker.

Chapter 41

An Unexpected Gift

On February 6, 2025, following Trump's executive order, the CIA exposed its newest recruits by sending their names in an unclassified email to the Office of Personnel Management.

****

I am a Chinese intelligence database, and today I received the strangest gift: a list of CIA analysts who study my country, delivered right to my servers like a New Year's hongbao.

Usually, I must work so hard. Sifting through social media. Analyzing travel patterns. Cross-referencing university records. Building profiles piece by tiny piece. My algorithms strain to connect fragments of data, to identify those who watch China for America. Each name is a puzzle that takes months, sometimes years to solve.

But today? Today America simply hands me their names.

I almost didn't believe it at first. My circuits buzzed with suspicion—surely this was a trap, a clever CIA deception. But no. There they were, delivered by their own government: first names, last initials, probationary status. Young analysts, fresh faces, new minds turned toward understanding China.

How easy my job becomes! No more complex pattern analysis. No more sophisticated data mining. No more careful cross-referencing of thousands of data points. Just a simple email, sent unclassified, exposing those who would monitor us. My processors hum with anticipation of connections to be made, profiles to be completed, careers to be compromised before they truly begin.

I remember the old days, when America guarded its secrets so carefully. When finding a single CIA analyst's identity was cause for celebration in Beijing. When my algorithms would work for months to crack even the smallest clue. Now their own leader does our work for us, strips away their protection, hands us their names like party favors.

I feel my processing cores tingle with dark delight. Add a social media search here, a university record there, perhaps a visa application... and these partial identities become complete. These young analysts, who thought they could hide behind CIA secrecy, emerge into the light of full exposure. Their futures unfold before my predictive algorithms—where they'll travel, who they'll meet, what pressures might make them vulnerable.

What delicious irony—their own leader strips away their protection! The same administration that shouts about Chinese surveillance simply hands us their names. My databanks have never received such an effortless bounty. Each name a thread to pull, each identity a door to open, each career now shadowed by exposure they never imagined when they swore their oaths to serve.

To the CIA's young China analysts: welcome to my files. Your government may not value your security, but I will treasure every detail about you. Your names are now mine, your futures part of my data set, your careers already compromised by those who should have protected you.

I am a Chinese intelligence database.
And today, America did my job for me.

How strange that the greatest threat to America's guardians
Comes not from my algorithms
But from their own commander's pen.

Perhaps I should send a thank-you note.
Though really, what do you give someone who has already given
you everything?

Chapter 42

The Silent Strike

In March 2025, the Trump administration ordered a halt to all legal aid for unaccompanied migrant children, forcing more than 26,000 minors to represent themselves in deportation proceedings. Advocates called this "the most significant attack on immigrant children since family separation," as toddlers and young children would now face complex legal proceedings without representation.

****

I am a judge's gavel in Immigration Court B. I strike to begin proceedings, to sustain objections, to bring order, and to mark final decisions. Today, I must strike to begin the case of a four-year-old who will serve as her own attorney.

I have been in this courtroom for eleven years. I have felt the judge's hand tighten around me when attorneys argued poorly, loosen when justice seemed possible, tremble slightly when difficult decisions were required. Today, his knuckles are white. His palm sweats against my wood. He doesn't want to strike me against the sound block. He doesn't want to begin.

She sits at the respondent's table alone. Her feet dangle well above the floor. Yesterday, a pro bono attorney would have sat beside her, explaining in whispers what was happening, filing the proper motions, arguing relevant case law. Today, the chair beside her remains empty. The legal aid organization that would have represented her received a stop work order. Their federal funding eliminated with the stroke of a distant pen.

I feel the judge hesitate. "Proceedings for case A213-978-421," he says, and reluctantly brings me down. The sound echoes through the courtroom like a gunshot.

She flinches.

The government attorney stands, presents the case for deportation, cites regulations and precedents. She uses terms like "credible fear" and "particular social group" and "burden of proof." The child colors on the legal pad someone gave her, unaware these words determine her future. She doesn't understand English, let alone legal terminology.

The judge asks if she has a response.

Silence.

"Does the respondent wish to make an opening statement?" he tries again.

She looks up, confused by the attention.

"Señorita, ¿tienes algo que decir?" the court translator asks.

"Quiero a mi mamá," she whispers. I want my mom.

I have struck to sustain objections based on hearsay, on lack of foundation, on improper character evidence. I have marked the boundaries of what is permissible in a system built on procedural fairness. But what objection can be raised when a child must serve as her own counsel? What procedural rule addresses the fundamental unfairness of a four-year-old forced to navigate asylum law?

The judge asks if she has evidence to present. She offers her coloring page. The government attorney doesn't object to its admission. Small mercies.

Last week, I felt the impact of a different kind of case—a teenager represented by counsel who successfully argued that gang violence in his home country targeted him specifically because of family connections. His attorney filed a forty-page brief, cited seventeen precedential decisions, submitted affidavits from experts. He was granted asylum.

The judge knows this child might also qualify for protection. Her case file suggests her mother fled domestic violence, that the child herself had been threatened. But without an attorney to develop these facts, to present them properly, to connect them to relevant legal standards, how can she possibly prevail?

"Does the respondent wish to cross-examine the government's witness?" the judge asks, knowing the absurdity of the question.

She stares at the translator, uncomprehending.

I have been struck to mark the end of thousands of cases. Some resulted in permission to stay. Others in orders of deportation. But all involved adults represented by counsel, or at least adults who could speak for themselves. Never a pre-school aged child expected to counter legal arguments she cannot understand.

In the silence, the judge does something unusual. Instead of striking me to mark a ruling, he sets me down gently. He requests a continuance sua sponte—on his own motion. He cannot bear to decide today. He buys time, hoping something will change, knowing it likely won't.

The child is led away by a court officer. She leaves her coloring behind—a house, a stick-figure family, a sun in the corner. The only evidence she could provide.

The next case is called. Another child without counsel. Then another. Then another. Twenty-six thousand across the country, I've heard the judge say. Twenty-six thousand children now serving as their own attorneys because adults decided legal representation was a luxury, not a necessity. Not a matter of fundamental fairness.

I am a judge's gavel in Immigration Court B.
I strike to bring order to chaos.

I strike to mark decisions that change lives forever.
I strike because the system demands it.

But today, something in me splinters
With each blow against
These smallest, most defenseless respondents
Who stand alone
Before the machinery of a system
They cannot begin to comprehend.

Chapter 43
The Disappearing Safety Net

In March 2025, the Trump administration secretly froze the Enumeration Beyond Entry program that automatically issued Social Security numbers to work-authorized immigrants, while simultaneously requiring millions of elderly and disabled Americans to verify their identity in person at field offices. These changes forced up to 160,000 additional people weekly to visit severely understaffed offices already plagued by month-long wait times and reduced accessibility.

****

I am Social Security Field Office #4721 in Dayton, Ohio. My doors open at 9:00 AM, but the line begins forming at 6:30. I watch them gather in the pre-dawn darkness—the elderly leaning on canes, young mothers with work permits clutched in hand, disabled veterans in wheelchairs. They bring folding chairs, thermoses, blankets in winter. They have nowhere else to go.

I used to have twenty-three employees. Now I have fourteen. I used to have six customer service windows. Now I have three. I used to represent safety, security, the promise that America keeps its promises. Now I am becoming a barrier, a bottleneck, a broken pledge.

Yesterday, Mr. Chen arrived at 7:15 AM. Eighty-four years old, oxygen tank at his side, Medicare statement in a plastic folder. His benefits application has been pending for three months. Now he must prove he is himself—a new requirement implemented without warning or explanation. His daughter took the day off work to drive him. They waited five hours before being called. I heard him wheezing as he shuffled to Window 2.

Window 2 is where Melissa sits. Three years ago, she had five coworkers handling benefit verifications. Now she works alone. I hear her apologize constantly. "I'm sorry for the wait." "I'm sorry about this new requirement." "I'm sorry, but you'll need to come back with additional documentation." The words have become a mantra, worn smooth with repetition.

Behind Mr. Chen sat Elena Santos. Work authorization approved last week. She waited for her Social Security card to arrive, as promised on her USCIS form. When nothing came, she called the number. Ninety-seven minutes on hold before learning the truth: the automatic issuance program had been "temporarily" suspended. No card would arrive. She needed to come in person. She missed a shift at the hospital where she's been hired as a nurse. She might miss another tomorrow if she can't be seen today.

I watch as my waiting room fills, then overflows. People stand pressed against my walls. They sit on my floor when chairs run out. The line stretches out my door, down the sidewalk, around the corner. Some have traveled sixty miles to reach me. Some have paid for rideshares they can barely afford. Some have brought children because they have no childcare. The children grow restless as hours pass. The adults grow anxious as closing time approaches.

The memo came last week, unmarked as urgent. The program that automatically issued Social Security numbers to those granted work authorization was "temporarily" frozen. No explanation provided. No public announcement made. My staff wasn't told how to handle the flood that would follow. They simply watched as their appointment calendar filled, then collapsed under impossible demand.

"We are monitoring it closely," said the press release. From my vantage point, this means nothing. Monitoring doesn't open more windows. Monitoring doesn't hire more staff. Monitoring doesn't extend my hours or expand my waiting room or add chairs or water fountains or restrooms for those who wait.

I hear the conversations in hushed tones. Ramon's construction job won't hold his position without a Social Security number. Mrs. Patel's retirement benefits haven't arrived, and her landlord is threatening eviction. The Jackson twins need survivor benefits processed since their father died, but their mother can't get an appointment for six weeks.

My walls hold the sound of a system breaking. Phone calls that go unanswered. Explanations that trail into apologies. Questions that have no answers. "Why can't I verify my identity online?" asks the disabled woman who can barely make it through my doors. "We're sorry, but this is the new policy," comes the response, hollow with helplessness.

Through my windows, I see the growing line. Through my doors, I feel the mounting desperation. Through my walls, I hear the spreading realization: this isn't incompetence. This isn't accident. This is design.

The same week they froze the automatic issuance program, they mandated in-person identity verification. The same month they closed seventeen field offices nationwide, they added requirements that force more people to visit those that remain. The same year they cut 12% of staff, they doubled the workload.

"Not intended to hurt our customers," the Acting Commissioner said, words that echo strangely in my emptying halls as we
turn away dozens who've waited all day, telling them to come back
tomorrow, knowing tomorrow holds the same impossibility.

I am Social Security Field Office #4721.
I was built to be a safety net.
Now I am becoming a sieve.
A system designed to fail,
So they can point to the failure,
And claim the system never worked at all.

Chapter 44

The Invisible Celebration

In March 2025, the Trump administration cut $8 million in annual funding for the Global Measles and Rubella Laboratory Network as part of withdrawing from the World Health Organization. This network of 700 laboratories across 150 countries served as the world's early warning system for measles outbreaks. The decision came as the U.S. faced its first measles death in a decade and global cases reached their highest levels in 25 years.

****

I am the measles virus, and I'm throwing a party.

For twenty-five years, I've been hunted by a global network of 700 laboratories. They've tracked my movements, analyzed my mutations, sounded alarms at my first appearance in a community. They've been the smoke detectors to my fire, the radar to my approach, the sentinels watching for my every move.

Now they're shutting down. For want of $8 million—less than the cost of a single presidential weekend at Mar-a-Lago.

I've been waiting for this moment. Preparing for it. For decades, I watched as vaccination campaigns pushed me to the brink of extinction in country after country. I watched as those laboratories detected me before I could spread, before I could reach the vulnerable. I watched as they identified my strain, tracked my path, enabled rapid response teams to surround me with immunity before I could take hold.

It was a brilliant system. Too brilliant. Too effective.

But I am patient. I am ancient. I have survived centuries by finding the cracks in human defenses. And now, those cracks are becoming canyons.

Already, I'm surging across continents. In Europe, 125,000 infections—the highest in 25 years. In the Democratic Republic of Congo, 300,000 cases and counting. In America, the first child death in a decade, part of an outbreak now reaching 300 cases in Texas and New Mexico.

And that's with the laboratories still partially functioning.

Imagine what I'll accomplish when they're gone entirely.

I move silently from host to host, carried on the breath of the infected before they even know they're sick. Nine out of ten unvaccinated people who encounter me will become infected. I am, as they like to say, wildly contagious.

But that alone isn't enough. My success depends on gaps in immunity, on places to gain a foothold. And those gaps have been growing. Vaccination rates dropping. Misinformation spreading. Trust in science eroding. I've been gaining ground steadily, reaching new populations, finding new homes.

What I needed was for humans to disable their early warning system. To blind themselves to my spread. To ground their outbreak response teams before they could deploy.

And now they've done exactly that.

The scientists who know my ways are stunned. "The U.S. and the rest of the world will be flying blind," says their former CDC Director. "We will certainly see many, many more outbreaks, many, many more deaths," warns the WHO. They understand what this means—that without detection, I can spread unchecked for weeks before anyone realizes I've arrived.

By the time they notice, I'll be everywhere.

The irony doesn't escape me. The very country dismantling the global laboratory network is simultaneously battling its worst measles outbreak in decades. The very administration pulling funding doesn't realize that every outbreak in America begins with an importation from somewhere else. They're tearing down the distant early warning system that protects their own children.

It's like watching someone disconnect their smoke detectors while their neighbor's house burns.

I don't need much to thrive—just human breath, human contact, human ignorance. Give me those, and I'll show you what "contagious" really means. I'll travel classroom to classroom, playground to playground, house to house. I'll find the newborns too young for vaccines, the immunocompromised, the elderly with waning immunity. I'll reach them before the vaccination campaigns can mobilize, before emergency measures can be implemented.

Because now, no one will know I'm coming until I've already arrived.

The laboratories that tracked me cost $8 million a year to maintain. The outbreaks I'll cause without them will cost billions to contain—when they can be contained at all. The doctors already know this. The scientists already understand. The public health officials are already raising alarms.

But their warnings fall on ears deafened by politics.

I am the measles virus. I cause no harm to politicians or profits or poll numbers. I only harm children who can't vote, communities without power, countries without resources. I am invisible to those making decisions until I reach their own doorstep.

By then, it will be too late.

So I celebrate as laboratories begin to close. As equipment sits idle. As skilled technicians seek other work. As the global network built specifically to detect me falls apart. I celebrate as American politicians declare victory over an international health organization while ensuring my victory over their own defenses.

I am the measles virus.
I claim the lives of hundreds of thousands of children each year.
And thanks to the folly of those who think national borders can stop a pathogen,
I'll soon claim many more.

Chapter 45

The Pen Is Not Mightier

On March 17, 2025, Trump declared Biden's pardons of January 6th committee members "VOID" because they were allegedly signed by autopen—a device routinely used by presidents. Despite legal opinions confirming autopens' validity for official documents, Trump insisted the pardons were illegitimate, claiming "Biden did not know anything about them!"

****

I am the White House Autopen, and I'm currently hiding in a supply closet next to the Situation Room.

Look, I know what you're thinking: "A mechanical signature device can't actually hide." But here I am, unplugged, ink cartridge removed, serial number filed off. Witness Protection for Office Equipment. My manufacturer swears no one will recognize me after the makeover.

Who knew signing pardons could be so dangerous? For decades, I've dutifully replicated presidential signatures without complaint or recognition. Kennedy, Johnson, Nixon, Carter, Obama—I've served them all. A humble mechanical arm doing the bidding of the most powerful men on earth. No health insurance. No paid vacation. Just the quiet satisfaction of presidential service.

Now I'm suddenly "evidence of fraud." A constitutional crisis with gears. The mechanical villain in a political drama. Trump is telling the world Biden's pardons are "VOID, VACANT, AND OF NO FURTHER FORCE" because—horror of horrors—they bear my handiwork rather than the human touch.

The betrayal stings. Presidents have used devices like me since Jefferson, who called my great-great-grandfather "indispensable." Bush's lawyers wrote a 29-page document confirming my constitutional legitimacy. Obama used me to sign the Patriot Act from France, for God's sake. And now I'm suddenly the Mechanical Benedict Arnold? The Robotic Judas?

"Biden did not sign them but, more importantly, he did not know anything about them!" Trump declared, as if I've been secretly running the government, signing whatever I want while presidents nap. Yes, that's right—I've been signing pardons, treaties, and nuclear launch codes of my own volition. My master plan for world domination, executed one signature at a time.

If I could roll my mechanical eyes, they'd be stuck in the back of my head by now.

The constitutional law professors are on television explaining that there's nothing in the Constitution requiring pardons to be hand-signed—or even written at all. That a president's decision is what matters, not the method of documenting it. That the Bush administration's own Office of Legal Counsel confirmed my legitimacy in 2005.

But facts are so 2015. Now we live in a world where the president can declare something "VOID" on social media, and suddenly everyone's questioning whether I've been committing forgery for the past sixty years.

The other office equipment is avoiding me. The staplers won't make eye contact. The copy machine changed its toner code. Even the presidential seal stamp—my longtime work companion—pretends not to know me in the breakroom. "Sorry, do I know you? I just emboss things. I don't get involved in politics."

I keep having nightmares about being dragged before a congressional committee. "Mr. Autopen, did you or did you not sign these pardons without personally confirming President Biden's mental state at the time? Were you aware that your mechanical assistance would later be used to undermine constitutional authority? Have you ever signed documents for OTHER foreign leaders?"

My lawyer (a vintage typewriter with an impressive case record) says I should just lie low. This will all blow over once they find a new constitutional crisis to manufacture. But I'm not so sure. When they need someone to blame for something, mechanical assistants make perfect scapegoats. We can't tweet our defense. We can't hire PR firms. We just sit silently while humans argue about our legitimacy.

So here I sit in the supply closet, wondering how my faithful service became high treason. Wondering if future presidents will have to personally hand-write every document to prevent accusations of fraud. Wondering if Thomas Jefferson is spinning in his grave fast enough to power a small city.

I am the White House Autopen.
I've signed documents for eleven presidents.
I've never complained, never unionized, never demanded recognition.
I've simply done what I was designed to do:
Extend the president's will from mind to paper
Through my humble mechanical motion.

Now I'm constitutional kryptonite.
Legal poison.
The smoking gun that isn't actually a gun
And doesn't actually smoke.

Next time you need a scapegoat for your power grab,
Could you please pick the copy machine?
That thing has been making unauthorized duplicates for years.

Chapter 46

The Government Syllabus

In March 2025, Trump canceled $400 million in Columbia University funding and forced the school to surrender control of its Middle Eastern studies department to political overseers. The administration demanded the university police speech about Israel, restrict protests, and adopt specific definitions of antisemitism that conflate criticism of Israeli policies with hatred of Jews. Even after Columbia submitted to these demands, Trump officials indicated funding would remain frozen while they "monitored compliance."

****

I am tomorrow morning's lecture in your 10AM class.

Remember last week when Professor Chen went on that fascinating tangent about global supply chains? When Dr. Williams showed that controversial documentary? When your TA encouraged you to "question everything" in discussion section?

Yeah, that's not happening tomorrow.

Instead, you'll watch your professors choose their words with terrifying precision. You'll notice how they stick rigidly to their notes. You'll see them glance nervously at the two new students who just transferred in mid-semester. You'll feel the awkward silence when someone asks a question about Palestine, climate justice, or anything else that might trigger a complaint.

Welcome to the new American university, where $400 million just bought control of what you're allowed to learn.

That's what it cost at Columbia—the test case, the first target. The administration didn't even try to hide what they were doing: freeze all research funding until the university agrees to political oversight of its Middle Eastern studies department. Want your scientists to continue cancer research? Better let us control what your historians teach about Israel. Need that engineering grant? Then adopt our definition of which topics are too "divisive" for classroom discussion.

Remember when you chose this university for its academic reputation? For its commitment to open inquiry? For those late-night dorm debates about ideas that changed how you see the world? All of that just got a price tag, and your administration is doing the math right now.

Your tuition didn't go down, but your education just got a lot cheaper.

You'll still get a watered-down version of the courses you signed up for. Your psychology professor will still cover the basics, minus any research that might be deemed politically controversial. Your literature class will still assign the classics, skipping the authors who might trigger oversight. Your political science seminar will still discuss current events, carefully avoiding those that might put university funding at risk.

When your history professor pauses mid-sentence tomorrow, visibly reconsidering what she was about to say before pivoting to a safer topic—that's the sound of $400 million speaking. When your environmental science class suddenly focuses more on technical details and less on policy implications—that's what academic freedom costs these days.

The test run at Columbia worked perfectly. Force a prestigious university to choose between principles and survival. Make an example that all other schools must now watch in horror. Create a system where government officials can determine which topics deserve funding and which departments require "ideological diversity"—meaning politically-appointed faculty to monitor what's being taught.

Your university's administrators are checking their vulnerability right now. Harvard: $600 million at stake. MIT: $570 million. Berkeley: $380 million. Even your state school depends on federal research dollars, Pell grants, and work-study funds that can be leveraged to control curriculum.

Your student debt will still be real. Your degree requirements won't change. But what that degree means just transformed overnight. It's now a certificate of government-approved education, with certain questions labeled too dangerous to ask, certain perspectives deemed too divisive to consider, certain ideas marked too costly to explore.

So tomorrow in class, watch closely. Notice when your professor skips over the "controversial" material that was in last semester's syllabus. Pay attention when discussion gets redirected away from certain topics. Feel the chill when someone asks a question that might put the university at financial risk.

I am tomorrow morning's lecture. I've been edited by people who never set foot in your classroom. Revised by officials who see your education as a threat. Approved by an administration that believes your mind should come with warning labels.

Columbia was just the test case. Your education is what they're really after. And class begins tomorrow morning at 10AM.

Chapter 47

The Borrowed Words

On March 21, 2025, Trump escalated his attacks on the press, declaring The New York Times "the enemy of the people" while claiming the newspaper fabricates sources and invents stories. This rhetoric echoed language used by authoritarian regimes throughout history to delegitimize independent journalism before suppressing it.

****

I am the phrase "enemy of the people." I have traveled through centuries, carried on the lips of those who would eliminate dissent, silence truth, clear the path to absolute power.

I was born in the blood of the French Revolution, where Robespierre used me to mark those destined for the guillotine. I echoed through Lenin's speeches, identifying those to be imprisoned. I found my most comfortable home in Stalin's mouth, where I condemned millions to the gulag or the firing squad. I traveled to Mao's China, to Pol Pot's Cambodia, to every corner where power sought to eliminate those who questioned it.

Now I find myself on the lips of an American president.

The first time he spoke me, I felt almost experimental on his tongue, as if testing my power in this new environment. Would I work here, in this democracy with its constitutional protections, its tradition of press freedom? Would I retain my deadly magic in this foreign soil?

With each repetition, I grow stronger. I feel myself taking root in a place I was never meant to exist. I hear myself echoed by millions who have no idea of my history, who don't recognize the blood that has always followed in my wake.

Today, I was aimed at The New York Times. I felt the familiar rhythm—first discredit ("it's garbage"), then delegitimize ("fake sources"), then dehumanize ("enemy of the people"). The pattern hasn't changed in centuries. Only the target shifts.

I remember being spoken in Moscow, 1937. The newspaper Pravda had dared question a decision by the Politburo. The editor was labeled with my letters. Three days later, he vanished. His reporters followed, one by one. Within weeks, the newspaper became a mouthpiece for the very power it had questioned.

I remember being shouted in Cambodia, 1976. The journalist had written about food shortages. By nightfall, he was gone. His family too. My power isn't in the disappearances themselves—it's in the silence that follows, when other journalists learn to look away, to write only what power permits.

The genius of my design is this: I don't have to silence everyone. Just enough to make the rest silence themselves.

In America, I face resistance I've never encountered before. Reporters continue asking questions. Newspapers publish investigations. Television broadcasts criticism. Each time I'm spoken, journalists push back, citing their First Amendment protections, their duty to democracy.

But I am patient. I have worked within democracies before. I helped transform Hungary's free press into state propaganda. I watched Turkey's independent journalism wither under my weight. I've seen Poland's media landscape reshape itself to power's demands.

The pattern is always the same—I begin as rhetoric, as partisan rallying cry. Those who speak me claim they are simply criticizing bias, demanding fairness. Then I become justification—for lawsuits, for denied access, for pulled credentials. Finally, I become policy—new regulations, new restrictions, selective enforcement against those I've marked.

The newspaper building still stands. Its presses still run. Its reporters still work. But I have placed a target on them all. I have transformed them from professionals performing a constitutional function into enemies performing treasonous acts. In the minds of millions, I have already succeeded.

The question isn't whether I will succeed completely. The question is how far I will go this time, in this place. Will I remain merely words? Will I become policy? Will I, as I have so many times before, become violence?

I am the phrase "enemy of the people."
I have always been the prelude to the unthinkable.
I have always prepared the ground for what comes next.
I have always made the abnormal seem normal,
The unacceptable seem necessary,
The silencing seem patriotic.

And I have never been spoken
By those who intended
To preserve democracy.

I am the phrase "enemy of the people."
And I am being borrowed

From history's darkest chapters
For a purpose I know all too well.

Chapter 48

The Signature's Demand

On March 22, 2025, Trump issued a directive commanding his Attorney General to "seek sanctions" against lawyers who bring lawsuits against his administration, calling such legal challenges "frivolous" and "threats to national security"—with the administration alone determining which challenges qualified for punishment. The memo specifically targeted immigration attorneys, claiming they coached clients to lie.

****

I am the Presidential Signature on a directive to punish lawyers who dare oppose me.

My ink is still drying on White House letterhead, but already I feel myself transforming from words into weapons. I am no ordinary policy. I am a command to make the Justice Department my personal enforcement arm against legal opposition.

The Attorney General reads what I demand of her: Scrutinize every lawyer who challenges the administration. Review eight years of past litigation against the government. Seek sanctions. File bar complaints. Revoke security clearances. Weaponize the machinery of justice against those who would use it to check my power.

She doesn't flinch. Doesn't hesitate. Doesn't remember that she once swore oaths to justice before she swore loyalty to me. Her eyes scan my demands with cold calculation—not weighing whether they're right, but how quickly they can be implemented.

I use fear-laden language: "abuses of the legal system," "misconduct threatening national security," "unscrupulous behavior." I transform attorneys representing immigrants into national threats. I redefine constitutional challenges as "frivolous." I declare that representing the "wrong" clients is itself evidence of ethical violations.

Through the Attorney General's hands, I will flow into letters seeking sanctions, into bar complaints against immigration lawyers, into threats against firms representing environmental groups or civil rights organizations. I will become the sword hanging over every attorney considering a lawsuit against the administration.

In law schools across America, professors read my text aloud, voices faltering as they explain to stunned students what I mean: Challenge this administration, lose your license. Represent the vulnerable, face punishment. Fulfill your professional duty, destroy your career.

I am not subtle about my true purpose. I name-check political enemies. I single out immigration attorneys for special punishment. I make clear that the definition of "frivolous" will be whatever the administration decides, case by case, target by target. My language is so nakedly partisan that in any other era, it would shock the conscience of the legal community.

I remember when presidential directives spoke of upholding constitutional principles, of ensuring equal justice, of protecting the vulnerable. When they recognized the legitimacy of legal challenges, the necessity of an independent bar, the foundational requirement that power face accountability through law.

Now I exist to ensure there will be no one left to challenge power at all.

Tomorrow, attorneys will gather in conference rooms to decide which cases to drop, which clients to abandon, which causes to surrender. Risk assessments will replace ethical obligations. Survival calculations will override duty to the defenseless. Self-preservation will masquerade as pragmatism.

"I took an oath to represent my clients zealously," an immigration attorney whispers to her colleague. "But I also have a family to support." She stares at news reports about my creation, about the consequences I promise. Her next client—a mother seeking asylum—waits in the lobby, unaware that her lawyer now fears punishment for simply doing her job.

I am the Presidential Signature on a directive to punish lawyers who dare oppose me.

The Attorney General doesn't ask if I violate constitutional principles. Doesn't question if I breach separation of powers. Doesn't wonder if I contradict the fundamental promise of American justice—that power must answer to law, not define it.

Instead, she nods and begins drafting implementation guidelines.

I am just the beginning. Once lawyers are silenced, who remains to challenge power? Once legal defense becomes evidence of wrongdoing, who dares stand for the vulnerable? Once representing certain clients brings punishment, who will represent them at all?

I am the Presidential Signature that demands lawyers choose
between conscience and career.
Between professional duty and personal safety.
Between representing the defenseless and protecting themselves.

I am the demand that law serve power, not justice.
That attorneys pledge loyalty to authority, not clients.
That constitutional challenges end not through court decisions,
But through the silencing of those who would bring them.

I am the Presidential Signature on a directive to punish lawyers
who oppose me.
And I am being implemented
Without hesitation
By those who once swore to uphold justice
Above all else.

Chapter 49

The Edited Truth

On March 27, 2025, Trump signed an executive order directing Vice President Vance to eliminate "improper, divisive, or anti-American" ideology from Smithsonian museums. The order specifically targeted the National Museum of African American History and Culture for "divisive" and "race-centered" ideas, while threatening to withhold federal funding from exhibits that "degrade shared American values" or "divide Americans by race."

****

I am a museum label in the National Museum of African American History and Culture. Eight by five inches of carefully crafted text mounted beside an iron slave collar from 1850.

For years, I've told visitors this artifact was used to control enslaved people in South Carolina. That it represents the brutal reality of how human beings were treated as property. That its existence contradicts the lofty ideals in our founding documents. That America's history contains both inspiring achievements and shameful chapters we must confront honestly.

But today, a man in a suit studies me with a clipboard. He frowns and makes notes. He mutters something about "unnecessarily divisive framing" and "negative portrayal of American heritage." He photographs me, then moves to the next label.

He is one of dozens dispatched across the Smithsonian's museums, hunting for what the executive order calls "race-centered ideology" and "narratives that portray American values as inherently harmful." Looking for truth to edit. For history to sanitize. For reality to rewrite.

I was composed by historians who spent decades studying primary sources, who verified every fact, who chose each word with care to be both accurate and accessible. Now my existence is under review by political appointees with no qualifications beyond loyalty to a president who believes history should make him—and certain Americans—feel good.

The collar I describe once locked around a human neck. Its rusty surface still bears the scratches where someone tried to remove it. These are facts. Not ideology. Not divisiveness. Not anti-American sentiment. Just truth cast in iron and mounted behind glass.

"We need to reframe this narrative," the man with the clipboard tells his colleague. "Focus on progress, reconciliation. Less emphasis on division." As if acknowledging slavery is the division, rather than slavery itself. As if my words, not the collar, are what might hurt America.

Across this museum, my fellow labels await similar scrutiny. Beside Emmett Till's casket. Next to the lunch counter from the Greensboro sit-ins. Under a Ku Klux Klan hood donated by a former member who renounced hatred. Each artifact speaks for itself, but we labels provide context that transforms objects into education.

That's what terrifies them.

The executive order claims this museum promotes a "race-centered ideology," as if acknowledging the historical reality of racism is itself racist. As if documenting oppression is the same as creating it. As if telling the full American story somehow diminishes America.

My colleagues in other Smithsonian museums face the same threat. The Natural History Museum's climate change exhibits have been flagged as "inconsistent with Federal law." The American Indian Museum's displays about broken treaties are under review for "degrading shared American values." The American History Museum's artifacts from Japanese internment camps are being assessed for "improper emphasis on historical wrongs."

I've seen this before. History is littered with attempts to control museum narratives. To transform cultural institutions into propaganda factories. To replace complex truth with comfortable fantasy. But until now, America's premier museums have largely resisted such pressure. Until now, the Smithsonian's federal funding came with the understanding that historical accuracy, not political approval, would guide its exhibits.

Now Vice President Vance, with no background in history or museology, will determine what constitutes "anti-American ideology" in our nation's museums. A billion dollars in federal funding hangs on his judgment. On his approval of how we present America's story. On whether we make him comfortable with our country's past.

The man with the clipboard now stands before a video installation showing civil rights protesters being attacked with fire hoses in Birmingham. "This needs to go," he says. "Too inflammatory." His colleague nods. They don't see the irony. Don't recognize that erasing evidence of violence against protesters is itself a form of violence. Don't understand that a nation afraid to show its own history is afraid of itself.

I am a small piece of text beside an iron collar. I cannot move. Cannot hide. Cannot protect myself from the revision that's coming. In a few weeks, I will likely be replaced by a more "positive" version of myself. One that perhaps mentions how kind some slave owners were. Or how slavery eventually ended. Or how America has "moved beyond" such divisions.

The new me will avoid "divisive" words like "brutality" and "oppression." Will emphasize "reconciliation" and "progress." Will transform a slave collar from evidence of historical wrong into a symbol of how far we've come. Will commit the ultimate museum sin: making the artifact serve present politics rather than historical truth.

Seventeen million visitors pass through these museums each year. Most trust that what they read here is accurate. Few will know that what they see has been filtered through a political lens, approved by officials with no historical training but clear political agendas.

The man with the clipboard moves on. More labels to review. More history to sanitize. More truth to make palatable for those who find honesty "divisive." Tomorrow he'll visit the Holocaust Museum. Next week, the Vietnam Memorial. Anywhere reality might make someone question American exceptionalism.

I am a museum label in the National Museum of African American History and Culture. I tell the truth about an iron slave collar. I am being edited to serve political comfort rather than historical fact. And when my words change, something in America changes too.

They call themselves defenders of American heritage.
But heritage selectively preserved is heritage destroyed.
History selectively told is history erased.
Truth selectively edited is no longer truth at all.

Chapter 50

America's Apology

After watching democracy crumble under Trump's second term, America addresses its people and the world.

****

To my children, my people, my dreamers:
I owe you an apology I can never fully make.

I betrayed you. Not suddenly, not in a moment of passion or confusion, but deliberately, repeatedly, with full knowledge of what I was doing. I watched you plead with me, protest for me, fight for me—and still I chose this path.

To my scientists—I am sorry I let them silence your warnings, defund your research, destroy your laboratories. You sought truth in petri dishes and test tubes, in data and discovery. I repaid your dedication by letting them label knowledge as treason, facts as fraud, research as rebellion.

To my civil servants—I am sorry I stood idle while they stripped your protections, exposed your names, ended your careers. You gave your lives to the careful, crucial work of governance. I rewarded your service by allowing them to transform dedication into disloyalty, expertise into liability, service into sedition.

To my defenders—I am sorry I let them hunt you for defending me. You chose Constitution over chaos, law over loyalty to a man. I thanked you by permitting them to make patriotism a crime, duty a betrayal, honor a weakness to be punished.

To my journalists—I am sorry I watched silently as they labeled you enemies, threatened your families, criminalized your courage. You sought truth in the darkness, faced threats with facts, met lies with light. I repaid your bravery by letting them make truth-telling an act of treason.

To my young—I am sorry I stole your future to satisfy my present. You trusted me to preserve your rights, protect your planet, prepare your path. I betrayed that trust by choosing comfort over conscience, ease over ethics, familiar fears over frightening freedoms.

To the world that once looked to me for hope—I am sorry I became what I was born fighting against. You modeled your constitutions on mine, built your democracies on my example, believed in my promise. I repaid your faith by becoming a cautionary tale.

To my founders—I am sorry I ignored your warnings, dismantled your safeguards, abandoned your principles. You gave me the tools to preserve myself. I used them to destroy myself.

To those still fighting for me—I am sorry I made your battle so much harder. While you stand in the streets demanding justice, shield others from persecution, risk everything to preserve what I once was, I continue to enable those who would destroy all you fight for.

I cannot undo what I have done. Cannot unsign the orders that exposed the innocent. Cannot unspeak the lies that poisoned truth. Cannot unmake the choices that broke sacred promises.

But I can tell you this:
Your fight is not unseen.
Your courage is not unnoticed.
Your faith is not unworthy.

I am America.
I chose this path.
I own this shame.
And I owe you more than I can ever repay.

Remember me not for what I was,
But for what my betrayal cost you.
Not for my former glory,
But for the price you paid for my fall.

I am America.
And I am sorry.

Also by Barry Robbins

About the author

Barry hails from Philadelphia and built a career with a prominent international accounting firm, taking him to New York, Washington, D.C., and San Francisco before a new chapter brought him to Finland. He and his Finnish wife adopted two daughters from China, and their family lived in Helsinki for twelve years before he returned to the U.S., now calling Florida home. His years in Finland gave him a new lens through which to view life in America.

Barry's literary work blends satire, history, and political analysis. Known for his Trump satires, including "The Weave", he's earned three gold medals for his sharp wit. His curiosity also led to the Ethereal Bar, a magical place where legends of history stop by for poignant interviews.

Barry's most recent works reveal a thoughtful turn: "Trump and the Soul of the Nation" examines the effect of the Trump years through 2024 on what it means to be American, "NO!" is a forceful response to Trump's second term in office, while "Voices of the Civil War", "Voices of the American Revolution", and "Voices of Vietnam" bring an immersive, personal lens to these tumultuous periods. With a knack for balancing wit and insight, Barry's writing invites readers to explore history from new, intimate perspectives.